Clash of the Sorcerers

Chronicles of the Library of Sorcery

Clash of the Sorcerers

Chronicles of the Library of Sorcery

Joan Marie Verba

FTL Publications
Minneapolis, Minnesota

FTL Publications
P O Box 22693
Minneapolis, MN 55345-0363
www.ftlpublications.com
mail@ftlpublications.com

Cover designed by Getcovers

Printed in the United States of America

ISBN 978-1-936881-80-2

Acknowledgments

I wish to extend my sincere thanks to Elizabeth Rowan Keith for her valuable advice and encouragement as I wrote this novel.

About the Author

Joan Marie Verba is an autistic author, publisher, and web developer with a bachelor's degree in physics. She was an associate instructor of astronomy for one year. She has worked as a computer programmer, web developer, editor, publisher, and social media manager. An experienced writer, she is the author of fiction and nonfiction books plus numerous short stories and articles. Her novels have received the Mom's Choice Award® and the Scribe Award. She is a member of the Science Fiction and Fantasy Writers Association and the International Association of Media Tie-in Writers.

To find out more about Joan, or to sign up for her newsletter, go to her website at https://joanmarieverba.com.

Introduction

Review of Book 1: *Secrets of the Sorcerers*

When Marlys was 16 years old, she went to a training center to learn how to become a sorcerer. She found the training methods harsh and cruel. These methods were tolerated, if not encouraged, by the High Sorcerer of the region, Thorne.

Marlys's sorcery awakened by accident when she was alone in the woods. Her sorcerer-trainer, Elspeth, realized that Marlys had become a sorcerer and brought Marlys to the High Sorcerer's fortress to introduce her. There, Thorne tested Marlys, first by challenging her to handle a behemoth, and then by stabbing Marlys to see whether Marlys could heal herself (she did).

Furious at this treatment, Marlys froze every sorcerer at the fortress in time and trained her own assembly of sorcerers in a gentler manner.

Twelve years after Marlys became a sorcerer, Thorne's niece, Nessa, appeared at the fortress, where Marlys now acted as High Sorcerer, and froze four of Marlys's friends in time in retaliation, refusing to release them until Marlys released Thorne and everyone else Marlys time-bound.

Realizing that Nessa had no intention of releasing Marlys's friends once Marlys canceled her time spell, Marlys refused.

Marlys and Nessa then separately began to search for a spell which would release a time-binding spell if the originator of the spell would not. While on the search, Nessa did her best to make Marlys's life as miserable as possible, hoping to force Marlys to release her spell on Thorne. This angered other sorcerers in other regions, and, as a result, Nessa was banished.

Both Marlys and Nessa realized that their only hope was to find the legendary Library of Sorcery. Clues to its location were said to be found in a line of sorcerer fortresses called the Spell

Passage. After gathering the information, Nessa reluctantly joined Marlys in the effort to find the Library of Sorcery, which they did.

Once at the Library of Sorcery, however, they found that a spell to cancel a time-bind that someone else had cast did not exist. This forced Nessa into an agreement with Marlys for each to release their respective time-binds at the same time.

That is where this novel begins.

Chapter 1

Once Marlys released the time-binding spell, her former colleagues started to come to life again. She noticed Serena casting a spell, but needed to keep her concentration on her predecessor, Thorne, who was in front of her. When Thorne began to look around, noticing a difference in her surroundings, Marlys knew it was time to speak.

Drawing herself to her full height and throwing her shoulders back, Marlys began her rehearsed speech.

"Some of you are noticing that this audience room contains more people than it did a second ago. I will explain." She turned to the two couples whose wedding had been interrupted first. "Bronwen, Fern, Skye, and Isador: Celestine will tell you what happened."

She lifted her chin. "To the rest of you, I am Marlys. I probably look different to you than when you last glanced at me. I cast a time-binding spell on you. You have been suspended in time for the past twelve years." She paused briefly, listening to the gasps and exclamations. Her attention, however, remained on Thorne.

Thorne glared at her sternly with keen hazel eyes. Her short gray hair framed her face, which had few wrinkles despite her age. "Why would you do such a thing?"

"That will become clear eventually," Marlys said. "Right now, I think it best that all of you who were time-bound become accustomed to your new environment. I am currently the High Sorcerer of Goldenvalley."

"You are not!" Thorne insisted.

Marlys kept Thorne in her line of sight, but continued to address the assembly at large. "There are sorcerers and apprentices near you who can escort you to your rooms and answer your questions."

"You did this to usurp my power," Thorne said. "You will not succeed." Thorne moved as if to cast a spell.

Marlys moved to counter, but a spell never landed.

Serena spoke up. "I cast a spell inhibiting the use of magic. No one here will be able to cast a spell here until I release mine."

Thorne turned her head. She glared at Serena. "You? A sorcerer? You're as thin as a reed! Look at your hands; your fingers are barely the width of a quill pen. A strong wind would blow you away."

The room erupted in laughter, though only among Marlys's assembly.

Tir took a step toward Thorne. "I think you'll find that Serena is the strongest sorcerer in this room, except for Marlys. Stronger than me, definitely."

Thorne scoffed. "You're a man."

"Correct!" Tir affirmed, pointing an index finger at the ceiling.

"You can't be a sorcerer!"

"Incorrect!" Tir responded, again, pointing a finger upwards.

Thorne swung around to face Marlys, who returned her stare evenly. "And you are not the most powerful sorcerer in this room."

Again, Marlys's assembly chuckled.

Undaunted by Thorne's attitude, Tir moved closer to her. "By now you must have noticed the aura around Marlys, and Serena, and me, as well as three others in this room. We've been to the Library of Sorcery. We are the most powerful sorcerers in this room."

Thorne glanced at Tir before turning back to Marlys. "The Library of Sorcery doesn't exist. It's a child's tale."

"No, Aunt Thorne," Nessa said, speaking for the first time. "There is a Library of Sorcery. We've been there."

Thorne turned to Nessa, eyeing her curiously.

Nessa ran up to Thorne and threw her arms around her. "I'm so glad you're back! I missed you so much!"

When Nessa released her, Thorne said, "Nessa?"

"Yes! I'm a sorcerer now. I'm not six years old anymore."

Zaria, Nessa's best friend, stepped forward. "You have Nessa to thank for your release. She and I went all the way to the Library of Sorcery to learn how to bring you back."

Marlys heard grumbling from her assembly, and raised a hand for silence. Now was not the time to remind everyone that Marlys had in mind to release Thorne and the rest of the time-bound sorcerers herself.

Serena walked up to Marlys. “I suggest that everyone in this room take an oath not to time-bind anyone else in this room, or we’ll have a cascade of retaliating spells.”

Thorne turned to Serena. “You suppressed the use of magic in this room, as I recall.”

Serena lifted an eyebrow. “I’ll release it to create a binding oath among us, and I’ll not restore the magic-suppressing spell after that.”

Thorne lifted her head and looked around the room. The audience room shone with the light streaming through stained glass windows. The polished floor reflected the light, and the high ceiling gave the room an airy feeling.

“Yes,” Thorne called out, “let’s have an end to this nonsense. We can all pledge not to time-bind each other.”

Marlys saw the members of her assembly turn to her. She nodded.

Serena turned and faced the assembly. “Everyone raise a hand.”

They all did.

Marlys felt Serena release her magic-suppressing spell.

“Repeat after me,” Serena continued. “I will not cast a time-binding spell on anyone in this room.”

All sorcerers and apprentices in the room repeated the oath.

Serena sealed the oath with sorcery, nodded to Marlys and Thorne, and moved back to where she had been standing earlier.

Thorne faced Marlys. The older woman stood a bit shorter than Marlys, but nonetheless managed to give the impression of filling the room. “Let me be clear: I am the High Sorcerer of Goldenvalley.”

Marlys gestured at the sorcerers facing them. “Half of the sorcerers here are pledged to you, yes.”

“As are you,” Thorne retorted.

“Am I?” Marlys said. “By tradition, a vacancy occurs when a High Sorcerer is unable to fulfill that role, and all pledges are void at that time.”

“A vacancy that you created, ungrateful wretch.” Thorne waved a hand toward the listeners. “We all came here to celebrate your ascendancy as a sorcerer, and this is how you repay us?”

“About that,” Marlys said. “I seem to recall your stabbing me with a knife.”

Thorne nodded. “A wound you instantly healed, proving your powers.”

“Unnecessary,” Marlys said. “I had more than demonstrated my abilities before that. Once I had healed myself, you bound me with an oath never to harm another sorcerer. Didn’t you take such an oath yourself?”

Thorne lifted her chin. “I took a different oath. I was bound not to harm another sorcerer oath-bound not to harm me. This was done so that I would be free to oppose a rogue sorcerer who never took that oath.”

“Therefore you are now bound not to do me harm,” Marlys said.

“Correct.”

“Good. Because we not going to start another sorcerous war over this.”

Before Thorne could answer, Elspeth, the senior sorcerer at the training center where Marlys had entered as an apprentice, walked up and touched Thorne’s arm.

“Thorne,” Elspeth said in a low voice, “I have been your friend ever since we were apprentices together. I have proved my loyalty to you. But we cannot erase what has happened. Marlys has taken the mantle of High Sorcerer here and half of the sorcerers here are pledged to her only. By their expressions, I can tell they aren’t willing to transfer that loyalty to you, at least not now. What Marlys says is true: we cannot start another sorcerous war.” She turned to Marlys for a moment and looked meaningfully at her before facing Thorne again. “Marlys shows no inclination to cast us out and has asked her assembly to treat us with courtesy. Let us relax in her hospitality, accustom ourselves to this time, and then there can be discussions.”

Thorne scanned the room, and apparently noticing all the expectant faces, turned back to Elspeth. “Yes. We cannot take any meaningful actions until we know what we are facing.” She turned to Marlys and added in a low voice, “This isn’t the end of this.”

Marlys raised her eyebrows. “I didn’t expect that it was.”

Thorne turned to the sorcerers and apprentices and raised her voice. “Those of you pledged to me, go with your fellow sorcerers here and refresh yourselves. I will give further instructions later.”

Marlys felt relieved to see her former colleagues start to leave with her current ones.

Nessa tugged at Thorne's arm. "Come, Aunt Thorne, I'll catch you up."

Marlys turned her back on them and walked down the steps of the dais to where the two couples she had been about to marry stood.

"I am sorry that your expected wedding has been delayed. We will hold the ceremony as soon as we can."

Skye turned to her. "I guess we missed quite a lot."

Celestine smiled and extended an arm. "If you'll come with me, I'll tell you everything."

The wedding party nodded to Marlys and followed Celestine.

"Wedding? Here?"

Marlys turned to see Thorne standing two steps behind her. Nessa held her arm.

"Yes," Marlys said. "Wedding. Granted, not many sorcerers have that wish, but when they do, I accommodate them. I don't force celibacy as you did."

Thorne scoffed. "Naïve girl. Never experienced the pain of a broken relationship, thanks to me. Sorcerers can't concentrate on their duties and attend to a spouse at the same time."

"I haven't noticed any problems among those already married," Marlys said. "Not every relationship ends in strife."

"So I thought when I was young," Thorne said. "I was so smitten I didn't even notice how I was being manipulated until it was almost too late. Just in time I realized that the man I thought was the love of my life only wanted me as a place to satisfy his rutting urges. I made sure that the rest of you would be spared that. You should thank me."

"I knew from a young age that any kind of coupling was not for me," Marlys said. "Most apprentices and sorcerers feel the same. So I can't see that what you did made any difference at all."

"Better to be sure now than have regrets afterward," Thorne said.

Marlys gestured at Nessa. "Your niece, who loves you, spared no effort to reunite with you. Why not sit with her for a while and find out what has happened in your absence?"

"Why did you time-bind me? Me, and everyone else in our assembly?"

Marlys lowered her eyebrows, drew herself up to full height, stood toe-to-toe with Thorne, and looked her straight in the eye. "Cruelty. I did it to stop your cruelty. Yours and all the other sorcerers in this region who felt cruelty was the way. I am happy to say I succeeded."

Thorne returned Marlys's gaze evenly. "You understand nothing." She turned and walked away with Nessa.

Marlys relaxed her shoulders. Serena, Tir, and Rochelle gathered around her.

Rochelle nodded toward Thorne's retreating back. "Yours is not an easy task."

Marlys shrugged. "I never expected it to be."

Serena stepped next to Marlys. "We will help in any way we can."

Marlys turned and smiled at them. "I know. But the main responsibility, and focus of her anger, needs to fall on me."

"We'll do our best to soften the blow," Tir said.

Marlys touched his arm. "Thank you. I appreciate your help."

Serena watched as Thorne turned a corner. "She will be surprised when she finds out what it means that we have been to the Library of Sorcery."

Tir folded his arms in front of him and grinned. "Didn't you hear? There's no such place."

"Didn't notice our auras?" Rochelle said.

"Oh, she noticed," Marlys said. "She's too strong a sorcerer not to have noticed. But like her niece, Thorne is too set in her ways to allow that to affect her."

"And like Nessa, she's going to run face-first into a hard, cold reality," Rochelle said.

Marlys nodded. "Then she will have to find a way to cope. I only hope that is sooner rather than later."

Chapter 2

The audience room emptied as members of Marlys's assembly escorted members of Thorne's company out. Marlys had noticed that Celestine had escorted the two about-to-be-married couples toward the dining hall, and followed. Tir, Serena, and Rochelle tagged along silently behind her. Although she welcomed their solicitation, Marlys wondered whether she would be needing a bodyguard while Thorne was around. Ahead of her, she noticed that Zaria was leading Nessa and Thorne to the dining hall as well.

The dining hall accommodated several long trestle tables. Celestine had already seated herself at once, opposite the two couples. A glance told Marlys that Thorne and her escort had taken a table farther away. She seated herself next to Celestine as Serena, Tir, and Rochelle settled beside her.

Bronwen turned to Marlys. "It seems that we missed a lot."

Skye grinned. "Yes, it's somewhat disappointing to have not been in on all the fun."

"It wasn't all fun, I assure you," Tir said flatly.

Celestine turned to Marlys. "We've resupplied and brought out all the decorations. We can resume the wedding as early as tomorrow."

"Do you think Thorne will let us?" Rochelle said.

"She can't stop us," Marlys said.

Tir swung around in his chair to look at Thorne. "Or, rather, we can stop her if she throws a temper tantrum."

"Throwing tantrums is not her way," Marlys said. "She tends to strike like a sudden bolt of lightning."

Serena turned to face Thorne briefly before turning back again. "We'll be on watch. She can't do anything we can't counter."

Isador smiled. "I thought being married to a sorcerer would be exciting. It seems I'm about to find out."

Celestine looked around at the group. "So, we're agreed that the wedding will be tomorrow?"

"I'm all for it if everyone else is," Fern said.

"Then it's settled," Marlys said. "Go ahead and make the arrangements."

The two couples stood.

"We'll be ready," Fern said, and left with Bronwen.

Isador and Skye followed, but took another exit from the room.

Tir looked toward Marlys. "I've cast the spell that Hilde taught us at Hilltop, the one which tell us where someone else is at all times." He inclined his head in Thorne's direction.

Marlys nodded. "I cast the same spell."

"I did, too," Rochelle said.

"And I," Serena added.

Celestine lifted an eyebrow. "I take it this isn't a standard locator spell, where you cast it once to find someone."

"This is a longer duration spell," Tir said. "Continuous."

"It's more precise, as well," Serena said.

"One of these days, you can teach it to me." After seeing the answering nods, Celestine stood. "Time to start gathering those on kitchen duty for the midday meal."

Marlys turned to the doorway where Skye and Isador had just disappeared, and saw Astrid walk in along with other sorcerers and apprentices.

Celestine met Astrid. "I thought we said that Thorne's assembly would be excused from kitchen duty for today."

Astrid gestured behind her. "They said they wanted to. It was their turn."

Marlys recognized Jana and Kelsie among the apprentices in Thorne's assembly who had joined Astrid. She walked up to them. "I expect you to be on your best behavior."

"Of course," Jana said innocently. "You're in charge."

Marlys exchanged a look with Celestine. She had already warned Celestine about Jana and Kelsie. Celestine responded with a nod indicating that she would stay alert.

Having accomplished all she needed to do at the moment, Marlys turned to Serena, Tir, and Rochelle. "I think I'll grab my pack and go to my room."

Tir grinned, "You mean yours and Thorne's."

Marlys nodded. “I know.”

“Need help?” Rochelle asked.

Marlys shook her head. “You need to get settled, too.”

“Call if you need us.” Serena walked away.

“By the way, I saw Astrid making off with our packs earlier,” Tir said. “They’re probably already in our rooms.”

“Thanks.” With a glance to Thorne, who seemed deep in conversation with Nessa and Zaria, Marlys left for her room.

When Marlys took over as High Sorcerer, she discovered that Thorne had a suite of rooms: two large ones with a spacious area in the middle, apparently a lounge and a study, plus an alcove partitioned in three sections: commode, tub, and vanity. One of the larger rooms had been Thorne’s bedroom. The other room, which Marlys had taken over, had sat largely empty except for a few well-upholstered and decorated chairs. Marlys guessed that Thorne had used this to relax or watch any happenings outside the fortress, since it featured a large window. Marlys had added a bed, dressers, and other personal items and had made this place her own.

Her carry bag had been set on a chair in the study. Marlys took it to her bedroom and began to unpack. She had been wearing the same clothes for weeks, cleaning them daily with household spells. The pants and shirt were comfortable, but she was glad she again had access to her entire wardrobe. After putting the clothes away, she put away her hairbrush, knife, and other daily implements. She still had waycakes, well-preserved. Those she placed on the tray resting at the top of her dresser. Last of all, she took out the key she had acquired along the spell passage. That she secured in a secret panel in the wall, guarding it with a spell. When the unpacking was done, she stretched out on the bed, resting.

Presently she heard a step and slid out of bed. She walked to the study and found Thorne standing there.

Marlys gestured to Thorne’s room. “Everything is as you left it.”

Thorne peered inside but did not walk in. “I see you kept it clean. I’m surprised you didn’t demolish it.”

“I had planned on releasing you eventually.”

Thorne faced Marlys. "How kind of you," she said dryly. "Do I need to move?"

"No," Marlys said. "But realize that I'm not moving, either."

"I hope you know that this is an impossible situation. One of us will have to leave, and it won't be me."

"Yes, I recognize the situation is impossible. Nonetheless."

Thorne glared at her. "You have no idea, child."

"Perhaps not. But I'm not a child anymore. I recommend keeping that in mind." When Thorne did not answer, Marlys said. "I'm going to go eat. Shall we walk together so that our respective assemblies know that we haven't started a war?"

Thorne threw her a sly look. "You have some sense after all, child."

Marlys ignored the diminution and walked out the door, Thorne beside her.

When they reached the dining hall, most of the assemblies had already seated themselves and began to eat, chatting merrily. Marlys noticed at once that the assemblies had not separated. Instead, most apprentices of both assemblies sat together. Sorcerers had clustered in small groups, but many had at least one member of the other assembly.

Thorne tuned to Marlys. "May we separate now?" she said with a sarcastic tone.

Marlys lifted an eyebrow. "You can sit wherever you want."

"How kind of you," Thorne said sardonically, and moved to a vacant seat near Elspeth.

Her usual group sat only a few chairs away. They had already begun buttering bread and tasting their soup. When Marlys sat in an empty chair—apparently reserved for her—Astrid walked over with a tray and served her.

"I see you remember my favorites," Marlys said.

Astrid smiled. "Of course."

"Though I can serve myself, you know," Marlys teased.

Astrid's grin grew wider. "I know. This is my pleasure." She walked away.

For a time, Marlys concentrated on eating, though she glanced around the hall to reassure herself that everyone was getting along. Since Thorne and Elspeth sat at the next table over, backs to her, Marlys occasionally caught bits of their conversation.

At one point, she heard Voni's voice. "Since I'm currently the senior sorcerer at your training center, Elspeth, I expect you to return, and we can talk about shared duties once we're there."

"That would be acceptable to me," Elspeth answered politely.

Marlys expected some sort of protest from Thorne, but instead she heard Thorne say, "As a senior sorcerer, you must know all the sorcerers in this area."

"Of course," Voni replied.

"This male sorcerer...," Thorne began.

"Tir, yes," Voni interjected.

"Tir," Thorne repeated. "How would you evaluate his abilities as a sorcerer?"

"As good as any," Voni said. "He specializes in spells of light and heat, and is the match of any sorcerer here, though I would guess that because of his stay at the Library of Sorcery, his powers have only increased."

"What about this Serena?" Thorne asked. "She seems to be too delicate and fragile to channel spells through her body."

"Many have said this to her prior to her coming here," Voni replied. "Since she has been here, she has proved herself many times over. You have probably heard already that we consider her the most powerful sorcerer here, after Marlys. In fact, she has developed several new spells."

"Such as?" Thorne asked.

"Her most notable spell is one that allows her to read speedily."

"How impressive," Thorne said dryly.

Marlys glanced at Serena, who said nothing, but whose expression indicated that she had heard and considered Thorne to be lacking in common sense. Tir, sitting next to her, had covered his mouth with his hand and turned his head to hide his chuckles.

Rochelle glared in Thorne's direction and began to rise from her chair.

"Sit down, Rochelle," Marlys said softly. "Now is not the time."

Rochelle complied.

Thorne said nothing else. The quiet caused Marlys to turn to see if anything notable was happening at the next table. Thorne had put down a fork and reached for a mug of cider. The mug moved out of reach. Thorne stretched out her arm and tried to grasp it again. Again, the mug moved.

Marlys pounded the table thunderously and stood. The room quieted. Looking around, she announced, “We do not play petty tricks on each other here. I expect all of you to treat your fellow sorcerers and apprentices with courtesy. That is all.”

A moment of silence followed. As Marlys surveyed the room, she heard replies of “Yes, High Sorcerer” or “Of course, High Sorcerer” or “It wasn’t me” or sounds of assent. Marlys sat, and dinner conversation continued. Marlys noted that a younger sorcerer sitting nearby, Esme, looked as if she were trying to shrink into her chair. When Marlys continued to face in that direction, Esme walked over.

Bending toward Marlys, Esme said softly, “I’m sorry, High Sorcerer.”

Marlys inclined her head toward Thorne. “I am not the one you need to apologize to.”

Thorne, seemingly aware of the exchange, turned in their direction and stood.

Marlys stood as well.

Esme stepped in front of Thorne, hands folded humbly in front of her, and bowed slightly. “I apologize, Sorcerer Thorne.”

“High Sorcerer,” Thorne corrected.

Esme glanced at Marlys, who nodded, and said, “I apologize, High Sorcerer Thorne.”

“I forgive you, child. How could you have known better?” Thorne said with a withering glance to Marlys.

Esme withdrew.

After exchanging determined looks, Marlys and Thorne sat again and returned to their respective meals. Marlys looked around occasionally, to reassure herself that no one else was plotting any mischief, but everyone seemed to be chatting sociably.

Marlys was finishing her tea and cake when she saw two apprentices of her old assembly approach Thorne and Elspeth.

“High Sorcerer Thorne, Sorcerer Elspeth,” one of them said enthusiastically.

Marlys saw Thorne visibly brighten at the title.

"There's going to be a wedding, here, tomorrow," the other apprentice said breathlessly. "Isn't that exciting?"

"I haven't been to a wedding since I left home," her companion said. "The food, the dances."

"We're all invited," the other apprentice said. "Can we come?"

Marlys braced herself for the possibility that Thorne might forbid it.

Instead, Thorne smiled. "Of course you can come. I had planned on coming myself."

The two apprentices bowed slightly. "Thank you, High Sorcerer," they said before scurrying away.

Elspeth turned to Thorne. "That was well done," she said approvingly.

"Wisdom," Thorne answered, "is knowing when to stand out and when to blend in."

Over at Marlys's table, Tir leaned toward Marlys and said in a low voice, "Do you think she might try to sabotage the wedding?"

"I am certainly not going to let her do that," Serena murmured.

Marlys looked from Serena to Tir. "She knows she will be watched, not only by us, but our entire assembly as well as hers. I'm not going let my guard down, but I think the wedding will go on without any interference from her. She'll confront us at a time and place of her own choosing."

"Since she knows we're not going to toss her out," Celestine said, "she has all the time in the world to plan."

"So do we," Serena said.

Chapter 3

The night passed peaceably in the High Sorcerer's suite, with Thorne retiring and closing the door to her room, and Marlys closing hers. The next day, after breakfast, wedding preparations, interrupted months earlier by Nessa and Zaria, continued apace. Those on kitchen duty cleaned up after the morning meal and promptly began to cook for the midday feast. Tir joined Isador in Isador's room and helped him with his wedding outfit while other sorcerers assisted Skye, Bronwen, and Fern with their wedding fineries in another room.

Marlys put on her most formal gown and walked around the main audience room. Sorcerers and apprentices had already festooned the columns and windows with flowers. The floor shone, the strip of red carpet dividing the room and leading to the high sorcerer's throne on the dais had been expertly cleaned. They had been blessed with a sunny day—light streamed through the high stained glass windows, illuminating the room in bright colors.

One or two or a few at a time, the sorcerers and apprentices trickled in, dressed in their finest clothes. Thorne walked in, wearing an elegant gown trimmed with jewels and embroidered in gold.

Marlys examined her own gown. Sparkling with silver trim and sequins, fashioned from the finest silks, it was every bit the equal to what Thorne wore.

Marlys noticed that Thorne did not even turn in her direction. Instead, Thorne walked among the sorcerers and apprentices Marlys recognized as her old assembly. From the gestures and tones of voices, the conversations were lighthearted and cordial. Marlys felt reassured that all would go well.

Eventually, the audience hall filled. Marlys kept an eye out for Nessa and Zaria. They were among the last to enter. Once inside the door, they leaned against a far wall as if trying to anonymously melt into it.

At last, the two couples walked in, all formally dressed, escorted by their attendants. They approached the dais, standing at the foot of the steps. Marlys climbed the stairs to stand at the top, in front of the High Sorcerer's throne. At that moment, Thorne ascended the stairs and sat on the throne, regarding Marlys calmly. Marlys said nothing, but stepped a few paces to one side. The wedding parties, below, also moved to stand just below Marlys.

Marlys drew herself to her full height and addressed the assembly. "Dear friends, we are gathered here in the presence of the Bright Beings and the Ruler of the Universe to bind together our beloved companions Isador and Sorcerer Skye, as well as our fellow Sorcerers Bronwen and Fern." She smiled at them.

They smiled back.

Marlys then recited the traditional words of the ceremony, asking each member of the couple to pledge to love, honor, and support each other through joy and adversity for the rest their lives. As she and the couples had planned, she started with Skye and Isador, then had Bronwen and Fern recite their vows. When each couple had pledged to their intended spouse, Marlys raised her hand in blessing.

"I now declare Skye and Isador married in mind, body, and spirit. I further declare Bronwen and Fern married in mind, body, and spirit. May the Bright Beings bless each union."

Each couple exchanged a kiss. The onlookers cheered. The air became alive with sparkling lights above, and tiny flakes of snow falling from the ceiling. Glancing around, she saw Tir directing the lights, and other sorcerers providing the snow, which melted and evaporated before reaching any of them.

Following tradition, the onlookers cleared a space for the two couples to lead the wedding dance. Tir ceased his spell-casting and picked up a lute, joining Rochelle and the other musicians among the sorcerers and apprentices providing the tunes.

Once the married couples had completed the first dance, others filled in the gap with traditional line and circle dances.

Marlys and others not inclined to dance moved to the edges of the assembly. Some watched, some conversed. Thorne kept her seat on the dais, as if presiding over the festivities.

Serena approached Marlys. Raising her voice slightly to be heard over the music, she said, "I don't feel comfortable with Thorne sitting there. Either you should be in that seat or the seat should be empty."

Marlys glanced to Thorne and then back to Serena. "She's not causing a disturbance. I'm inclined to leave her there."

"The symbolism is hard to miss," Serena said.

"Sitting in the chair doesn't make her the acting high sorcerer, any more than if Isador sat there."

Serena chuckled. "Still. The smile on her face isn't entirely benign."

"Trying to remove her, though, would create a scene which would only make me look bad," Marlys said.

"I see your point," Serena said, "but the intention is clear. She is not going to give up her claim to the title easily."

Marlys took a breath. "I don't expect it to be easy. But I do expect to prevail."

"You have a plan?" Serena said.

"Yes. Just as we did with Nessa and Zaria, I plan to let her find out on her own that her goal is not achievable."

Serena sighed. "It took a long time for Nessa and Zaria to come to that realization. I may take longer for Thorne to come to the same conclusion."

"I have time," Marlys said.

When the dancing ended, Marlys led the way to the dining hall, followed by the married couples, followed by everyone else. Those on kitchen duty had set up two tables next to each other in the front of the room for the couples. Everyone else sat at the long tables for the feast. During that time, those who had not already extended their congratulations in the main hall came to the tables and added their good wishes.

When the main meal had been cleared, and the sweets and delicacies served, the traditional speechmaking began. After that, each couple came to Marlys for a final blessing.

"I wish all of you joy." Marlys said. Nodding at Skye and Isador, she said, "You're escaping to the inn at Valleyview for your honeymoon, as planned?"

Isador smiled.

"As soon as we change and get our things, we'll slip away," Skye added, before leaving with her husband.

Marlys turned to Bronwen and Fern. "Still going to Safe Harbor?"

They nodded. "Yes. We were going to shorten the distance and take a few days for the journey, but Rochelle offered to escort us directly there using the spell you learned at the Library of Sorcery. It is her birthplace, where she grew up, after all."

Marlys smiled. "When you return, you can settle in to your own training center and start teaching apprentices. Eventually, we'll have spells that we learned at the Library of Sorcery to share."

"Don't too much while we're gone," Fern said. "We wouldn't want to miss anything."

Marlys chuckled. "We'll make sure that you are caught up."

Bronwen and Fern smiled before taking hands and scurrying away.

When they had gone, Marlys surveyed the room. Half of the seats were empty...all of her old assembly. Her current assembly lingered over sweets, conversing.

Curious, Marlys slowly walked to the back of the room, taking the exit to the audience chamber. There she saw her old assembly standing in front of Thorne, backs to her. Thorne faced in her direction but seemed to take no notice.

"Nothing's changed," Thorne said in a reassuring voice. "I'm still in charge. I'm still High Sorcerer here."

"But what do we do now?" Kelsie said.

Thorne turned in her direction. "Go back to your training centers." She looked around the room. "All of you. Apprentices still need to be trained, their sorcery awakened."

Janna crossed her arms in front of her. "They say there's a new way of awakening sorcery now."

"Try it if you wish," Thorne said. "It will work or it will not. When it does not, they may reconsider. In the meantime, there is still sorcerous work to be done in this region. Cooperate with the other sorcerers and apprentices. They've been instructed to treat us kindly. Outdo this kindness, if you can. We are not starting a sorcerous war, and any conflict would only reflect badly on me."

"What are your plans?" Elspeth asked.

"I will remain here and claim what is mine by right," Thorne said evenly. "It may take time, but eventually it will become plain to everyone that I'm the one to continue to be High Sorcerer in Goldenvalley." She raised her head. "Don't you think so, Marlys?"

Everyone turned to face Marlys.

"I bear no ill will to any of you," Marlys said. "Thorne is correct in that you can return to where you were twelve years ago in safety and security. Your possessions have been preserved. Your rooms are ready for you. And yes, those who recognize my leadership are pledged to cooperate with you and treat you kindly."

"When do we leave?" Elspeth asked.

"Everything is ready for your departure," Marlys said. "If you gather your things together, you could leave as early as this afternoon, if you wish. You can approach the members of my assembly who were with you when the time-binding spell ceased."

Everyone turned back to Thorne.

"Go with my blessing," she said. "There are always the sorcerous channels if you need to reach me."

The assembly dispersed. Thorne and Marlys remained in their places. As she passed Marlys, Elspeth touched Marlys's elbow briefly before walking on.

Marlys only nodded in response, feeling Thorne's gaze upon them.

When only Marlys and Thorne remained in the chamber, Marlys approached the elder sorcerer. "That was well done."

Thorne's brows lowered. "I have no need of your praise," she said coldly. "Our rules and customs may have allowed you to preside here, but I am the elder sorcerer in this region I did not give up my throne. Remember that."

"I can give you my promise I won't forget," Marlys said. "But, I, too, have duties that I cannot easily put away or transfer to another."

"We shall see." Thorne turned away promptly and walked toward the rear exit of the chamber without another word.

The departures began almost at once. Marlys left the fortress to bid farewell to members of her old and new assemblies.

Elspeth was among the last to leave. Janna and Kelsie had already boarded their wagon, excitedly talking about resuming their sorcerer training.

After a long look back toward the fortress, Elspeth approached Marlys. "After some reflection, I wanted to say that I wish things had gone differently between us. Thorne and I grew up together, did household spells together, trained at the same center. She convinced me that harsh methods were the only way, and my experience with training apprentices only seemed to confirm that. I could tell upon arrival that you had great potential. I let Janna and Kelsie have their way, thinking their rough ways would push you into awakening your sorcery. And then, somehow, I saw that you had awakened it on your own. I wanted to ask you about that, and would have if you hadn't time-bound us."

Marlys nodded. "I realize I didn't give you the opportunity."

"Voni and I have talked," Elspeth continued. "She told me your story, how your sorcery awakened, and the sacrifices you made to rebuild an assembly in Goldenvalley. You have earned your position. I, for one, am looking forward to learning the new way of training."

"Thank you."

Elspeth turned toward the fortress again. "Your task won't be an easy one. Thorne will fight to restore her position."

"I know that."

"I wish I could stay and help, but I can't. There's still a bond of friendship between Thorne and me, and she could use that as leverage against you. It's better for you that I leave, though if I can help distantly, I will do what I may."

"I'm grateful for the offer."

"May the Bright Beings be with you." Elspeth turned to climb aboard the wagon.

"And with you," Marlys called after her.

When the last of the wagons disappeared due to the distance-shortening spell, Marlys stood by herself. Those of the assembly assigned to the fortress started to return there. Serena, Tir, and Rochelle stood at a respectful distance, talking among themselves.

Nessa and Zaria approached Marlys.

"I guess this is home, now," Zaria said. "What do you want us to do?"

"Celestine hands out the assignments here," Marlys said. "You can speak with her. I think you and Nessa have the rest of the day to yourselves, though."

Nessa shook her head. "This is nothing as I imagined."

"Oh?" Marlys queried.

"Somehow I thought that when I released Aunt Thorne from the time-binding spell, there would be a joyous reunion between us. We'd speak of old times and resume our family ties."

"What happened instead?" Marlys asked.

"She pelted us with questions..." Nessa began.

"Lots of questions," Zaria emphasized.

"...about what had happened, who was running things, what were you like," Nessa said.

"Along with complaints about how unfair this was and what an upstart you were," Zaria added, "and didn't you know you were pledged to her, even though that pledge was technically broken."

"She didn't even thank me," Nessa said, "even though I explained all that I did for her, the umbrage I faced, even banishment from the regions, all for her." She looked Marlys in the eye. "I overheard her confess, in her own words, that she did stab you, and she sounded proud of it."

"I am sorry," Marlys said. "Quite often, events don't unroll as we imagined or hoped they would."

"Talking to your assembly," Nessa said, "what they told me about Thorne, confirmed everything you said about her. I hardly recognized my aunt from their description. I felt as if I wanted to melt into the walls and stay there."

"We even used the sorcerous channels to talk to sorcerers in other regions," Zaria said. "They confirmed what you already said about Thorne."

Nessa glanced to the fortress before facing Marlys again. "I feel embarrassed to walk among your assembly. They know what I did, they know what my aunt did, they know that we're related."

"I don't think they'll judge you for that," Marlys said. "Think of it as a fresh start."

Nessa turned from Marlys to Zaria and back again. "We're grateful for that."

Zaria added, "And promise that we won't betray you again."

"Even without casting a truth spell, I believe you," Marlys said.

"My aunt is another matter," Nessa said. "She will oppose you with every ounce of power she has."

"Leave her to me," Marlys said. "This is now my problem. I will deal with it." She smiled. "Besides, having been to the Library of Sorcery, any of us is a match for her power now."

"Thank the universe for that," Zaria said.

"Don't underestimate her cleverness," Nessa said. "What she lacks in power she more than makes up in cunning."

Marlys nodded. "I'm prepared for that, too." She put a hand on each of their shoulders. "Besides, with you two added to my team, how can we fail?"

Chapter 4

The dining hall seemed almost empty that evening, with only ten sorcerers and a half dozen apprentices sitting at the end of a long table. Thorne dined alone, two tables over, and seemed unbothered by the fact that even Nessa and Zaria sat with Marlys and the other residents of the fortress.

Tir looked over at Thorne. "What is it that she's reading?"

Celestine looked up. "Oh, that's the journal of daily activities here." She turned to Marlys. "She asked for it, and I couldn't think of a reason not to give it to her."

"I wouldn't put it past her to shred it," Rochelle grumbled.

"That's why we keep two copies," Marlys said.

"It's going to be a long read...twelve years of records," Serena said, "and she doesn't know the useless speed-reading spell that I developed."

Tir grinned. "I think she's going to find out that your spell is not so useless."

"At least it will keep her occupied," Astrid said.

"Don't count on it," Nessa said wearily. "She's capable of holding multiple thoughts in her mind at once."

Marlys smiled. "Fortunately, that is a talent that most of us have."

After dining, Thorne picked up the book and left her plates behind.

Rochelle turned to Marlys. "Was she that way before you time-bound her?"

"I don't know," Marlys said. "The only time I saw her here was when I time-bound her, and we never got around to the celebratory feast."

"I have been to many centers," Serena said. "Sometimes the High Sorcerer pitches in with the everyday work. Other times the High Sorcerer does only the sorcerous and administrative tasks, and others do the cleaning up and putting away."

"I'll clear her plates." Nessa took a tray, put her dishes on it, and walked over to the other table.

"For that matter, I've left my plates on the table for others here many a time," Marlys said.

Astrid stood and began to clear their table. "Yes, but you don't *expect* us to do it for you. We take on tasks for you because we *want* to."

"And because we're on kitchen duty," Celestine added.

"I thank you for all of it," Marlys said.

"I don't think we can expect any thanks from Thorne," Tir said.

Rochelle faced Marlys. "Are you going to be all right in that suite of rooms tonight? I'm a little nervous with the thought of you being alone and so close to Thorne."

"Rochelle, I have an entire arsenal of protective spells I can use," Marlys said. "I'll be fine. I was fine last night."

"Last night Thorne was still recovering from the time-binding spell," Serena said, "and the fortress contained an abundance of sorcerers to call upon if needed."

"As a precaution," Marlys said, "I cast a spell before sleep that will awaken me if anyone or anything comes near. I won't be taken by surprise."

Tir snapped his fingers. "How disappointing. I was counting on sleeping outside your door tonight."

They all laughed.

When Marlys reached her—and Thorne's—suite of rooms that evening, she found Thorne continuing to read the record book.

Thorne looked up as Marlys walked behind her. "I left the doors open. We're pledged not to harm each other. It's friendlier that way."

"I generally leave the doors open in case someone needs to find me," Marlys replied.

Thorne nodded and returned to her reading.

Marlys could have cleaned herself by sorcery, or even household spells, but felt the need for a bath. She undressed in a corner of her room, out of Thorne's direct sight, put on a robe, grabbed a towel, and walked into the bath area. There she did shut the door. Thorne made no sounds of protest.

When Marlys emerged, she walked to her room, shed her robe, slipped on a nightgown, and sat at the desk opposite her bed. There she was in full sight of Thorne, but Thorne remained intent on her reading.

Marlys made an entry in her journal of the day's activities, and then turned to Celestine's record of the happenings in the region while she had been away seeking the Library of Sorcery. Celestine had thoughtfully left the book on her desk.

She had not reached the end of the notes when she sensed a spell being cast near her. Turning, she saw Thorne accessing the sorcerous channels. For a moment, Marlys thought of shutting the door to give Thorne some privacy, but then concluded that if Thorne wanted privacy, she would have closed the door herself or gone elsewhere in the fortress to cast her spell. Marlys resumed her reading.

"Ilse!" Thorne said, referring to the High Sorcerer of the nearby Meadowlands region. "It's been a long time. More than twelve years, I understand."

"Too long," Ilse replied. "I had hoped that Marlys would release you well before now. The younger sorcerers conveyed the news to me yesterday."

"Yes, I suppose that the sorcerous channels have been active since my release. Half the continent must have been informed by now."

"It is a significant event," Ilse said. "One we all have been waiting for."

"Now that I have returned, I am taking up my post again as High Sorcerer of Goldenvalley."

"Oh? Did Marlys step aside?"

"Not precisely, but she will see the wisdom of it, especially if I have the support of other High Sorcerers such as you."

"I recognized you as High Sorcerer before Marlys time-bound you."

"Of course, you will do so again."

"I have recognized Marlys as High Sorcerer these past twelve years. As far as I'm concerned, she's the current High Sorcerer, and there is no change. Voluntarily or not, your post was vacated."

"But that's what I mean. It was not voluntary."

"Vacated is vacated."

"But...!"

"Let me tell you the same thing I told Marlys. I am not getting involved in any disputes not of my region. If you have a quarrel with Marlys, you will have to work it out with her."

"But she is not stepping aside. Surely you see...."

"Your niece, Nessa, was banished from my region and all the others precisely because she tried to force the issue. I understand from the younger sorcerers that Marlys reprieved her for the Goldenvalley region. That is her affair. Nessa is still unwelcome here and at all the other regions, and if you wish to avoid the same fate, I would recommend that you not stir up any trouble yourself."

"But you always supported me in the past."

"Yes. But the past is past. This is now. I can understand that from your point of view that you have stepped into an entirely different world than you experienced just a few days ago, and that this is distressing to you. But that's as far as my sympathy goes. Welcome back, and good night."

Silence followed. A very long silence. Marlys had heard the entire conversation, as Thorne had undoubtedly intended because she had been confident that Ilse would enthusiastically back her up. Marlys did not look toward Thorne through the door opening, but she listened. No sound of weeping, gnashing of teeth, or other distress. She had a fleeting thought of extending some empty pleasantry to Thorne, but realized in the next moment such an action would be interpreted as capitulation. That she would not do. Stepping down as High Sorcerer would betray Serena, Tir, Rochelle, and all the other sorcerers in her assembly. She would not do it.

Eventually, Marlys sensed Thorne casting another spell.

"Ware!" Thorne said cheerily.

"Welcome back, Thorne," Ware's voice said. "The sorcerous channels have been buzzing with the news of your revival."

"Thank you. I wanted to talk to you about the seat of the High Sorcerer here at Goldenvalley."

"I had been thinking about that, too, since I heard the news," Ware said.

"You have?"

"Of course. How wonderful it must be for you to be able to finally retire."

"Retire?"

"Yes, retire. We all saw how much effort you put into making Goldenvalley a great region. Since I ascended here as High Sorcerer, I know the work, the worries, the complications. It's stimulating to me now, but I foresee the time will come when I'll gladly allow another qualified sorcerer to take my place."

"I'm not ready to retire!"

"Thorne, we all saw how you aged over the years. The strain must have been tremendous. What a blessing that you have someone like Marlys to assume all those onerous duties. You will be free to study, to mentor the young sorcerers, to train the apprentices. You might even find time for yourself."

"But I'm not ready to give up my post. Indeed, I was hoping you would support me in helping me keep it."

Ware's voice went from cheerful to stern. "Thorne, you know that no sorcerer anywhere wants to start a sorcerous war again."

"I'm not planning to do that, but...."

"Good. Neither I nor anyone else is going to get involved in any internal dispute you have in Goldenvalley. You would be wise to take my advice and retire. That is the action that would have all of our support."

"All?"

"I can safely say, all. My best wishes to you for a long and restful residence there. Good night."

Another long silence.

Presently, Marlys sensed Thorne reaching out again.

"Lindra! Good to see you."

"I heard you were back," Lindra said matter-of-factly.

"Yes, and ready to resume my duties as High Sorcerer of Goldenvalley."

"Did something happen to Marlys?"

"Nothing happened to Marlys. She's sitting at her desk in her room next to me right now."

"She relinquished her title?" Lindra asked skeptically.

"No, she has yet to see the wisdom in that," Thorne said. "But you were always my supporter in the earlier days."

"That's true, but I was your supporter because there was no other choice. Most of the other High Sorcerers went along with your ways for that reason. We were not comfortable with your manner, nor did we approve."

"You never said anything," Thorne said. "No one did."

"I regret my cowardice now."

"Cowardice? Cloverdell thrived under you. Your region had the most sorcerers among all of us."

"And the most casualties. I wrapped two apprentices in sailcloth to take them home to their families for burial. One tortured herself to death, trying to awaken her sorcery. The other took her own life in despair after none of her attempts to awaken her sorcery worked. I'm sorry to say that all my efforts at trying to save them failed. I will regret that for the rest of my life. When I heard that you were time-bound, and that Marlys was awakening sorcerers by kinder methods, I put them into practice immediately and never looked back. We're now thriving as never before."

Marlys heard a brief silence before Thorne continued. "I am sorry for your losses. We all have had them. I have felt every single one of them. Deeply. But no one said awakening sorcery would ever be easy. It wasn't for me. I know it wasn't for you, either. You must remember how many times we tried gentler methods. We failed."

"The harsh ones failed just as often."

"I can't believe that you supported Marlys in time-binding me, either. This was an affront to my office. An act of impudence. An act of rebellion."

"It was just a matter of time before a determined sorcerer with sufficient strength came along to oppose you. If it hadn't been Marlys, it would have been someone else. I thought of doing it many times myself, but I couldn't think of how to do it without violating my oath not to harm another sorcerer. Although time-binding occurred to me, it also occurred to me that sooner or later, I'd have to release you, and where would I be then?"

"But you found the wisdom not to do it."

"Or failed to find the backbone to do it. I wasn't the only one. Other sorcerers, in my region and others, secretly tried to think of ways to depose you. We even thought of going through the Spell Passage to reach the Library of Sorcery. Our records showed a sorcerer in our area actually reached it, many lifetimes ago, and came back with stronger powers. It was said that she could light up the sky."

"I'm afraid you'd find the Spell Passage disappointing. Minor spells such as calling sheep. Climbing walls. Listening to singing crystals. Baking cakes. That's all I learned when I was there. I even reached the Mountains of Wrath. They're impassible."

"And yet, by your own admission there's a sorcerer in the room next to you more powerful than you can possibly imagine."

Thorne laughed derisively. "I have yet to see it. An aura alone does not make one's magic strong."

"Oh, I'd wager anything that you will yet see her power. And I would give anything to watch."

"What you will watch is me regaining my place as High Sorcerer here."

"I'd wager nothing on that. The younger sorcerers here are calling me for our evening revelry. Good night."

The silence stretched even longer this time. Most sorcerers kept to a schedule of using the sorcerous channels to early evening, unless there were urgent matters to discuss. It was still a reasonable hour to talk to one or two more sorcerers, but Marlys heard nothing more.

The conversation with Lindra had been interesting. She had spoken to Lindra before, on regional sorcerous business, many a time. After Marlys had time-bound Thorne and the others and started establishing her own assembly, Lindra apologized to her for not helping her out in those early days. Marlys had easily forgiven her...she had not really expected help, and had been afraid to ask for it, fearing judgment for the time-binding. But the other High Sorcerers had welcomed her pleasantly, if hesitantly.

She had not known until this moment, however, that others had been thinking of displacing Thorne. If she had known, she would have felt much less isolated, both as an apprentice and as a young sorcerer. Their fear of Thorne, even time-bound, must have been strong.

Marlys closed her journal. She had long since kindled a sorcerous light so that she could write. She pushed back her chair, stood, donned a robe over her nightgown, and walked into the next room. Thorne sat back in her chair, unmoving, staring at the wall. This room, too, was lit by sorcery.

When Marlys reached a point in crossing the room where Thorne could easily see her, Marlys looked back. “I’m about to go to the kitchen to get some tea. Would you like me to bring some for you?”

“Hm,” Thorne said, as if rousing herself from a reverie. “Yes, I’d like some tea.” She made no eye contract with Marlys, however.

“I’ll return soon.” Marlys walked out of the suite.

Chapter 5

Marlys met Rochelle coming out of the kitchen as she was going in.

"I was about to find you," Rochelle said. "I've heard from Bronwen and Fern."

"Oh? How is the honeymoon going?"

"They're enjoying the oceanside region, but they told me that officials in the area were going door-to-door to warn everyone to be on alert in case they had to evacuate. It seems there's a volcano in the islands rumbling and casting out lava. The sorcerers there think it may be nothing—such things happen on a regular basis in the islands—but it's best to be prepared for a possibility of a tsunami."

"There hasn't been one in quite some time, has there?"

Rochelle nodded. "Not in my lifetime, at least. My grandparents told us of a huge ocean surge when they were youngsters. Then, too, sorcerers on the islands, who had just endured a tsunami there, warned the seacoast communities in plenty of time to move to higher ground. They said the sight of the tsunami was something they would never forget."

"I don't doubt it, from descriptions I've heard."

"And how is Thorne? Behaving herself?"

"So far. Using the sorcerous channels to try to find allies."

"Has she succeeded?"

"Not so far. She left the doors open, probably thinking that I'd overhear other sorcerers rallying to her cause. Instead, she's had quite a shock. I left her sitting staring at the walls."

"Forgive me if I say I don't feel a bit sorry for her."

"That's understandable," Marlys said. "Any sympathy from me she'd mistake as weakness."

"Do you feel sorry for her?" Rochelle asked.

Marlys shook her head. "Not overly so, not after all she did. She's facing the consequences of years of her actions. Still, I'm not about to return nastiness for nastiness."

"I wouldn't sink to her level, either. Good night, and good luck."

"Thank you." Marlys continued to the kitchen as Rochelle walked away. Heating a kettle of water with sorcery was a simple, quick action. She found a clean empty teapot, cups and saucers in the cupboard, small cakes in the pantry. She filled a tray and walked back to her suite.

Before she reached it, she heard Thorne's voice and stopped.

"I'm not a monster, Elspeth."

"Did anyone say you were?"

"No, but the implication was clear." Thorne sighed. "Didn't I treat the sorcerers well?"

"You did."

It was the apprentices that bore the brunt of the abuse, Marlys thought.

"I saw to their needs, celebrated their accomplishments, even Marlys had a celebratory gathering. She was the one who ended it."

With good reason, Marlys thought.

"True," Elspeth said.

"Didn't I make Goldenvalley prosper? Our harvests were good, our land was the most peaceful in the regions."

Except for the poorest of the poor, who were neglected and exploited, Marlys thought.

"You did," Elspeth said.

"I was respected."

You were feared, Marlys thought.

"You were."

Thorne sighed again. "They say I was harsh, but life is harsh. I wish it weren't, but it is. We have to deal with the world as it is, and it doesn't respond to a gentle touch. It responds to power."

Depending on how the power is used, Marlys thought.

"Why not get a good night's rest," Elspeth advised. "Morning may bring new insights."

"I wish it would bring insights to *them*. They can't see that they're doomed to failure."

Marlys almost laughed. *Twelve years of failure? Hardly.* Marlys would match her record of accomplishments to any other High Sorcerer on the continent.

"If so, you'll be there to remind them."

"I intend to. Sleep well, Elspeth."

After a long silence, Marlys continued toward the door to the suite. When she entered the study, Thorne turned. She remained seated, but reached for the tray as Marlys walked by.

"I'll take that."

Marlys continued walking. "Since I brought the tray, I'll serve myself tea in my room and return in a moment."

Thorne scowled but did not impede Marlys's progress.

When Marlys had poured herself a cup of tea and placed a couple of cakes on a napkin, she returned to the study and set the tray on Thorne's desk. "I take it you would prefer to serve yourself?"

Thorne looked up at her. "Do you consider yourself powerful beyond all imagination?"

Marlys smiled. "No. But my sorcerous powers strengthened at the Library of Sorcery, and I expect that my powers are the match of any sorcerer on the continent."

Thorne poured herself a cup of tea as Marlys talked. She took a sip. "It will be interesting to see them demonstrated."

"Since we sorcerers exercise our powers on a daily basis, I would expect others to notice, sooner or later."

Thorne took another sip. "Sooner or later. Hm."

Marlys did not reply, but turned and left the room. Thorne did not extend the conversation further, much to Marlys's relief. Marlys did not feel she had to prove anything to Thorne. Thorne would find out soon enough on her own how powerful a sorcerer Marlys was.

When only the resident sorcerers were at the fortress, breakfast food was laid out buffet-style on one of the tables or on the kitchen counters. Marlys would only have to place a plate, cup, and utensils on a tray and move the tray along the table, taking or pouring whatever she wanted.

Thorne was not there at the time Marlys, Tir, Serena, and Rochelle ate breakfast with Nessa and Zaria. Marlys saw her enter soon after, and to Marlys's surprise, Thorne joined them, sitting next to Tir.

Tir raised his eyebrows momentarily but said nothing and returned to eating breakfast. He faced away from Thorne but otherwise did not move from his seat.

There had been little conversation up to that point. Thorne took advantage of the silence and spoke up. “You know, you’re only the second male sorcerer I have seen in my lifetime.”

Tir looked at her. “Oh? Who was the first?”

“A nasty brute by the name of Argent. Somehow, he escaped the notice of the High Sorcerers and had awakened his sorcery, which he used to ill purpose. Theft, assault, and arson were the least of his infamous crimes. You think that my apprentice training was harsh? This villain was committing real atrocities. We found out about him when his victims came to us for healing.”

“I presume you dealt with him speedily,” Zaria said.

Thorne nodded. “At the time, it was traditional for the High Sorcerer to reserve a sorcerer for the purpose of dealing with such a rogue. My High Sorcerer selected me and bound me only to refrain from harming another sorcerer who had taken the oath not to harm another sorcerer.”

“Clever,” Tir said.

“What did you do?” Nessa asked.

“I opened a portal to the island worlds,” Thorne said. “Sucked him right in. Then I closed the portal and he was gone.”

“Marlys showed the technique to us,” Rochelle said, “but few of us have tried it ourselves.”

“It is reserved only for the worst of the worst,” Thorne said.

“When I was younger,” Marlys said, “before I became an apprentice, there was a band of men—not sorcerers—who terrorized my home region. Murder, theft, arson. My father, who was the magistrate, sent for a sorcerer to deal with them and she sent them to the island worlds. I had thought about becoming a sorcerer before, but when I heard this, I wanted to learn sorcery and protect the regions.”

Rochelle said. “That takes care of the problem here, but what about those in the island worlds? Are they being terrorized by those sent from here?”

“I neither know nor care,” Thorne said.

“When I opened the portals to show how it’s done,” Marlys said, “you could see that the island worlds have blue sky and green grass. It seems a habitable place. But I have read nothing that indicates that anyone is born there."

"For that matter, I haven't read anything that indicates that the island worlds have settlements," Serena added. "Either here or in the Library of Sorcery. Legends say that no cities or towns are there, but since no one has ever returned from there, there's nothing to confirm the legends."

"I think it is a measure of justice if the island worlds only have criminals preying on each other." Thorne turned to Marlys. "I'm surprised that you only demonstrated how to open a portal. I sometimes tested the strength of sorcery of newly awakened sorcerers by seeing if they could open one, or resist one once opened."

"You didn't let any be sucked in, did you?" Rochelle asked, scandalized.

"Of course not. I would close the portal before they were dragged in if they were too weak to resist."

"Marlys had us stand at a safe distance to watch, away from the maelstrom," Tir said.

"Hm," Thorne said as she picked up a teacup. "I suppose that one can learn spells by watching." She took a sip.

"Yes," Serena said confidently. "One can."

Marlys finished the piece of buttered bread she had been eating and faced Thorne. "I had a question for you."

Thorne's face broke out in an insincere smile. "Of course. It is my task to impart wisdom."

Marlys ignored the implication. "Why were the spells to complete a transition so well hidden? We had to make a thorough search to find one when Tir and his parents arrived here."

"And we had been to more than one sorcerer fortress," Tir added.

"Isn't it obvious?" Thorne said. "You don't want a naïve, first-year sorcerer changing the gender of an infant because the parents wanted a girl but had a boy, or vice-versa. You only want to use such a spell when there is a genuine need."

"You could simply locked the instructions away with a spell that required two or more sorcerers to unlock it," Marlys said.

Thorne shook her head. "This is not a spell to be used lightly. The more effort involved to find it, the more thought must go into applying it."

"Still, it needs to be available when it is necessary to use it," Marlys said.

"When you have been a High Sorcerer as long as I have, you'll appreciate that mine is the wiser way," Thorne said.

Some of the others opened their mouths to respond, but Marlys made eye contact and shook her head slightly.

They all returned to eating their breakfasts.

Fortresses generally stood on hills. The Goldenvalley fortress had been built at the top of a rise with a steep slope downward where it met the main road at the bottom. A cobblestone path lay between the fortress entrance and the main road.

At mid-morning, after attending to their regular daily duties, Marlys, Serena, Tir, and Rochelle walked halfway down the hill to talk away from Thorne. The air on this late autumn day was warm, the breeze still, the sky clear and brilliant. Trees had long since shed their leaves. Dry leaves of red, gold, and yellow covered the grass, and crunched beneath their feet.

"My, how she brags," Tir said, with a glance to the fortress.

"It's not having the desired effect," Rochelle said, "which I presume is to convince us how competent and powerful she is."

"...and how much better a sorcerer she is than Marlys," Serena added.

"Empty words," Marlys said. "Let her talk."

"It is annoying, though," Tir said.

Marlys nodded. "My guess is that she's still feeling stung by the rebuffs she received last night talking to the other High Sorcerers."

"Trying to enlist their aid in getting back her former post?" Rochelle guessed.

"Exactly so," Marlys said.

"Let me guess," Tir said. "None of them supported her."

"...which seemed to surprise her," Marlys said. "Ware tried to coax her into retiring."

"Ha!" Rochelle said. "I'd wager that didn't go well."

"It didn't," Marlys said.

Serena glanced back toward the fortress. "Here she comes."

"Do you think she knows we're discussing her?" Rochelle said.

"Probably," Marlys said, "but I doubt that she knows exactly what we're saying."

"Shall we ignore her and see if she'll just walk by?" Tir said.

"I'm in favor of that," Rochelle said.

They kept their backs turned to her and talked about the harvest in Goldenvalley, which Celestine had reported was abundant. Marlys felt, rather than saw, Thorne come within arm's length, and stop.

Marlys fell to the ground and felt herself being dragged. Immediately, she cast an anchoring spell to keep her in place. Leaves rose into the air and slapped her face as they rapidly flew past her. Turning to one side, she saw Rochelle and Tir also hugging the ground. Turning to the other side, she saw Thorne resisting the gale as she admired the portal she just opened.

Finally able to roll to one side and look up, Marlys saw Serena standing tall, seemingly unaffected as leaves, grass, and debris sped around her. She cast a spell. Marlys saw the round portal entrance slowly turn so that the full force of the atmospheric maelstrom concentrated on Thorne.

Thorne fell on her stomach, clawing the ground in a vain effort to stay in place. Feet first, the portal wind dragged her slowly to its threshold. Thorne screamed in frustration. Painfully, slowly, she managed to roll over, lift her arms, and close the portal just before it sucked her through.

The wind ceased immediately.

Thorne managed to sit on the ground, breathing heavily.

Marlys, Tir, and Rochelle got to their feet.

Serena, who had never even leaned to one side, brushed leaf debris from her clothing. She walked over to Thorne and looked down at her.

"It is unwise," she said, "to measure the strength of a sorcerer until you have regularly seen that sorcerer at work." She walked back toward the fortress.

Thorne looked up but said nothing.

Tir stepped up to Thorne. He smiled. "She stands up pretty well to a stiff wind, don't you think?" He followed Serena.

Rochelle took a turn. "Remember that useless speed reading spell? She read half of the books in the Library of Sorcery." She hurried to catch up with Tir and Serena.

By the time Marlys reached her, Thorne's breathing had returned to normal. She reached down. With a shake of her head, Thorne reached up and allowed Marlys to pull her to her feet.

"What? No cutting remark?" Thorne said.

"I can't think of any at the moment," Marlys said.

Thorne glanced in Serena's direction. She had stopped within a few paces of the fortress's entrance, and was speaking with Tir and Rochelle.

"I didn't know you could do that," Thorne said.

"Turn a portal?" Marlys said. "No, I didn't know you could do that, either. But as Rochelle said, she read fully half of the books in the Library of Sorcery."

Chapter 6

Thorne began walking slowly back to the fortress. Looking in that direction, Marlys saw sorcerers and apprentices at the windows and entryway, undoubtedly drawn by the sound of the hurricane-force winds. She followed Thorne, noticing that the ground, as well as the scattered trees, has been stripped of leaves.

When Marlys caught up with her, Thorne, continuing her progress, gestured at Serena. "I still don't understand how someone that delicate could become a sorcerer. There's hardly anything to her."

Marlys raised her eyebrows. "She's not as vulnerable as she seems. I've seen her defend herself capably. She walked to Goldenvalley all the way from Majesticacres, just to become a sorcerer. Every other sorcerer training center, even her family, told her she was too fragile for the training."

"Majesticacres?" Thorne said. "I thought she was from Silvervale."

Marlys shook her head. "Majesticacres. Her family is in the bookbinding business."

"They were not wrong, turning her away," Thorne said. "No reputable training center would accept someone for an apprenticeship who did not appear strong enough for the trauma of an awakening of sorcery, no matter what their facility was with household spells. People died, you know, and whatever else you think of me, we did try to prevent that."

"I have found that the strength of the body is less important than the strength of the mind. How many talented sorcerers have been missed all these years when those who seemed weaker were passed over?"

Thorne stopped and stared at Marlys for a few moments before speaking again. "What happened to you? We provide apprentices with good food, soft beds, sturdy roofs over their heads, elegant clothes. Even apprentices receive the greatest of respect from the citizenry. Why rebel?"

"Kindness would have helped."

Thorne snorted. "How did your sorcery awaken? You never said. Did you stub your toe?" she added sarcastically.

Marlys laughed. "I was trapped in a clutching bog and needed to awaken my sorcery to escape."

Thorne's expression changed to one of grudging respect. "You never would have escaped any other way." She took a breath. "You are not going to add that you didn't feel searing pain, I hope, because I would not believe you."

"No, the pain was excruciating. I was weak for days afterward, though I did my best to hide it from Elspeth and the others."

Thorne threw her hands up. "You know, if you had said something, you would have been warmly welcomed. We had a celebration all planned for you, a feast. I and the others were ready to embrace you as a sorcerer in our ranks."

"You threatened me with a behemoth. You stabbed me in the side."

"I had no idea how your sorcery awakened. Elspeth didn't see it. She said that you seemed to have created a portal to the island worlds, but there was no other evidence."

"So you didn't know whether I was or was not a sorcerer. If not, you could have killed me."

"Please. If you had not turned back the behemoth, I would have. If you had not healed yourself, I would have."

"Pardon me if I didn't see it that way at the time."

Thorne started walking again. "I do not. Pardon you. I was ready to elevate you to the senior ranks of sorcerers in this area, and you threw it all away."

Marlys matched Thorne's pace. "I was not about to spend the rest of my sorcerous life among those who tolerated cruelty in their ranks."

"There it is again. You just admitted your awakening was a traumatic event. It is only through pain that we reach the rank of sorcerer, child."

"Pain, yes. But it does not have to come through cruelty." When Thorne did not answer immediately, Marlys continued.

"Do you remember what you told me when you welcomed me into the rank of sorcerer?"

"I said several things."

"I seem to remember," Marlys said, "that you told me that you, too, were so angry at the way you had been trained, that when you awakened your sorcery, you nearly opened a portal to get rid of your colleagues."

"Yes, I said that. I'm surprised you didn't think of it yourself."

"Oh, I thought of it," Marlys said, "but time-binding seemed to me to be the better way."

"You would have failed to draw us through the portal," Thorne said. "Just as I would have if I had tried it."

"That occurred to me as well," Marlys said. "Time-binding had less of a chance of failure."

Thorne stopped again the faced Marlys. "Pity that you didn't learn from that."

"Learn what?"

Thorne continued to walk again, and Marlys with her. "I was young and naïve. Like you were…like you are. Elspeth and I thought we would reform the entire region. But we learned. We learned that we couldn't become sorcerers unless we accepted the pain and suffering we were told we must endure to awaken our powers. Our trainers almost sent us home. But we complied, and we became sorcerers.

"Then we were sent out into the regions to do the sorcerous tasks required of us. We found that we had to deal with theft, sloth, avarice, laziness. Such people don't respond to niceness, Marlys. They respond to a strong punch in the gut. Elspeth and I learned. We became hard. We ruled with a strong hand. And we got results. We maintained order and calm in this region. People respected us. It wasn't what we wanted. It was what we had to do."

"They did not respect you; they feared you," Marlys said.

"Is that so bad?" Thorne said. "Have you done better?"

"What I found," Marlys said, "is that genuinely lazy people are few. Most become productive when they're adequately housed, clothed, fed, and given worthwhile tasks to accomplish. Theft has diminished as well."

Thorne scoffed. "We never starved anyone! Or took their clothes, or damaged their houses."

"No, you punished them for their perceived failings without finding out what caused them to fail in the first place. We took the time to get to know them. If you go out among the people of Goldenvalley now, you'll find that nearly everyone is satisfied with how they are living. Sorcerers are greeted with genuine cheerfulness rather than wariness."

"How much you have to learn," Thorne said. "But no matter. I intend to stay here with you and look forward to the day when you realize from your failures that my way is the only way."

"You may have to wait long," Marlys said.

They had neared the fortress entrance by then. Thorne left Marlys and walked inside. Marlys strode to where Serena, Tir, and Rochelle had gathered.

"What was that about," Rochelle said, "if you don't mind my asking."

"The usual," Marlys said. "Her way is right, and my way is wrong, and I will eventually come to see things her way."

Tir chuckled and shook his head.

"How long do you intend to put up with her?" Serena said.

"I can't very well exile her," Marlys said. "She's done nothing wrong since I released her from the time-bind. I think it's best that she wants to stay here, where we can watch her and counter any threatening moves."

"I see your point," Serena said, "but that means we will have to be on our guard at all times, and that can become tiresome."

"Only I have to mind her," Marlys said. "I've accepted that. It's a consequence of my actions. But the rest of you, if you want to spend days, a week, even a month, at another training center or another region for that matter, you have my blessing. You could even visit a station along the spell passage if you wish. I'm sure they'd be glad to see any of us again, and get an account of what we've accomplished since we left."

Tir scratched his head. "That's an idea. But for now, I think I'll stay."

Serena and Rochelle nodded in agreement.

Marlys intended to go back to her room and rest for a while, but when she reached the door of the suite, which was open, she ran into a barrier. The impact did not hurt, but blocked her nonetheless. After confirming that this was a spell, she smiled and walked back to the audience room and through the common rooms, where Celestine was giving a summary of upcoming tasks to the sorcerers and apprentices.

"Sorry to interrupt," Marlys said.

Celestine turned to her. "Not at all. We're always happy to see you."

Marlys gestured. "Come outside and I'll show you a new spell. Serena, I presume you wrote the climbing spell in our spell book." When Serena nodded, Marlys added, "Would you mind getting it and bringing it out to the wall underneath my window?"

"Gladly." Serena hurried away.

Marlys led the way out, sorcerers and apprentices chattering excitedly behind her. Learning a new spell was always an event.

When they reached the spot underneath Marlys's main bedroom window, she turned to the assembly. "This is a spell we learned at the Overlook fortress along the Spell Passage. It's one they teach their newly awakened sorcerers, so any of you sorcerers can use it, and the apprentices have something to look forward to doing themselves when they become sorcerers."

While Marlys spoke, Serena strode over with the spell book.

"Serena, would you do the honors and read the spell?" Marlys said.

"Of course," Serena replied.

The assembly gave Serena their rapt attention as she read.

When Serena finished, Marlys said, "Now, let me demonstrate." She faced the wall, looked up, put herself in the correct frame of mind, cast the spell, and started to climb. Her audience gasped in delightful surprise as she ascended, as if climbing an invisible ladder.

Marlys drew even with her bedroom window. Another spell opened the window from the inside. Marlys climbed in and looked down. "See? Easy."

The onlookers applauded.

"I'll take them to the other side of the fortress where they can try it, too," Serena called up.

"Please do," Marlys said. She waved and closed the window.

Looking toward her open bedroom door, she saw Thorne walk out of her room and into the study, apparently curious about the noise from outside. She spotted Marlys, drew back her head in surprise, swung around toward the suite's entrance, tested to see that her blocking spell was still in force, and turned back to Marlys.

"How did you get in here?" Thorne asked.

Marlys grinned. "Magic, of course."

Thorne had removed the blocking spell by the time of the midday meal. She left for the dining hall shortly before Marlys did, and again joined the others at the table, but said little. Marlys could not help but notice, however, that she kept stealing glances at Nessa and Zaria, who were either ignoring her or oblivious to her attention.

Celestine and most of the other sorcerers and apprentices left the table first. Marlys, Tir, Serena, Rochelle, Nessa, and Zaria remained, as did Thorne. Eventually, Nessa and Zaria took their trays to the kitchen, then walked back through the dining hall and out the door leading to the audience chamber. Thorne rushed after them, leaving her plates and utensils behind.

"Nessa! A moment!"

Marlys could hear Thorne through the open door. A glance around told her that Serena, Tir, and Rochelle also showed interest in eavesdropping.

"Yes?" Nessa said, not sounding overly enthusiastic about engaging her aunt in conversation.

"You and Zaria reached the Library of Sorcery, did you not?"

Zaria's voice spoke next. "I thought you didn't believe in the Library of Sorcery."

"It's difficult not to, now that I've seen the evidence. I am not so foolish as to discard facts."

Marlys heard Nessa inhale sharply. "Yes, Aunt, we were there. What of it?"

"I could not help but notice that your sorcery was strengthened as a result."

"It was, yes," Nessa said.

"Can you tell me how to get there?"

"Absolutely not," Nessa said. Marlys heard two sets of retreating footsteps.

"Wait!" Thorne said. "A moment, please!"

The footsteps stopped.

"I went through the Spell Passage. I just couldn't get past the Mountains of Wrath. I only need for you to tell me the last step."

"Never," Zaria said. "We earned our way to the Library of Sorcery. If you wish to reach the Library, you will have to find a way yourself, as we did."

"We are not," Nessa added, "simply going to take you there, either."

"Whatever happened to loyalty? To family?" Thorne said.

"Our loyalty is to Marlys, without whose help we would be exiles," Zaria said.

"I had hoped we would be as family again," Nessa said. "Especially after all the sacrifices I made to release you from your time-bind. But I have only seen you wanting to take from me, not give."

"What of the love I gave you as a motherless child?"

"For that," Nessa said, "I will be eternally grateful. If that Aunt Thorne came back, I would consider her family. But that is not you now, and I have more than repaid my debt to you by seeing to your release. You will get no more from me."

Marlys again heard two sets of footsteps retreating.

"Ingrate," Thorne called bitterly.

Neither Nessa nor Zaria answered, and the footsteps faded away.

Not long after, Thorne walked through the door into the dining hall again. When she drew even with the others still sitting there, Tir said, "We aren't telling you, either."

Thorne picked up her plate—with only food leavings remaining on it—and threw it against a wall, shattering it.

"There's a limit as to how much we will clean up after you, too," Marlys said.

Thorne glared at her.

Slowly, Marlys pushed her chair back and drew herself up to her full height, meeting Thorne's stare evenly.

Thorne stared at her as if seeing Marlys for the first time. This puzzled Marlys—she had done nothing more but straighten her posture and stretch herself as far as she could go—but she kept her pose.

After a few moments, Thorne turned away, silently cleaned up the pieces and the resulting mess sorcerously, then stalked out of the dining hall.

Marlys relaxed and turned to her friends, who also stared at her.

"How did you do that?" Tir asked.

"Do what?" Marlys said.

Serena gestured at Marlys. "In addition to your aura, there was a nimbus around you, especially surrounding your head and shoulders."

"Anyone would be able to see that," Rochelle said, "not just sorcerers."

Marlys pulled back a chair and sat. "I did no more than what I might do if someone in the towns or farms was being stubborn or recalcitrant, to impress them...just kindle small sorcerous lights near me...like the sparkles that you and the others provided for the wedding."

"It was more than that," Tir insisted.

Marlys let out a breath. "I wish I could tell you what I did, but I can't, since I didn't do it deliberately."

"I didn't read all the books in the Library," Serena said, "though I read a great many of them. I didn't come across this."

Tir smiled and snapped his fingers. "Drat. I'll have to try to imitate that by myself, then."

Chapter 7

That evening, after dinner, Marlys sat in the desk in her bedroom, writing in her journal, when the image of Voni appeared in her room.

She put down her pen and sat back. "Voni," she said, acknowledging the sorcerous communication.

"Can we speak privately?"

Marlys nodded. "Thorne is taking a walk on the grounds."

"Good," Voni said.

Elspeth's image joined Voni's. "Marlys. We thought you would be interested in how Janna and Kelsie are adjusting to their new associates."

"At your instruction," Voni said, "I briefed the apprentices I had before you came back and warned them that Janna and Kelsie might make mischief."

"They'd never try anything against a sorcerer, of course," Elspeth added.

"How did the apprentices take it?" Marlys asked.

Voni smiled. "They thought it was the delightful challenge of a lifetime. I saw them huddling in corners, making plans."

"So Janna and Kelsie have been behaving themselves?" Marlys said.

Elspeth smiled. "Your memory is failing you if you think they had any such intention."

"What happened?" Marlys queried. "I presume something did."

"In the middle of the night, I heard an apprentice shout, 'Rally!' Immediately, the apprentices' sleeping area lit up with lights generated from household spells, and the chimes at the windows rang softly. Elspeth and I crept over to see an apprentice kneeling on her bed, with a line of apprentices standing on the floor between her and Janna and Kelsie. The defending apprentices just stood there, arms crossed in front of them, as if daring Janna and Kelsie to make a move."

“Did they?” Marlys asked.

“They giggled as if making a joke and went back to bed,” Elspeth said. “Then the other apprentices returned to their beds, and Voni and I returned to our rooms.”

“Have they tried anything since?” Marlys asked.

Voni smiled. “No. In the morning, we heard a pounding on the door. Seems that the other apprentices gathered together and took Janna’s and Kelsie’s beds outdoors during the night with Janna and Kelsie still in them.”

“What happened then? Mutual retaliation?” Marlys asked.

“Strangely, no,” Elspeth said. “It seems that, at least for the moment, they’ve reached a tacit understanding. They all gathered as a group and quietly listened as Voni and I gave them their lessons and assignments for the day.”

“They actually eat together as one group and work together fairly well,” Voni said.

Marlys let out a long breath. “My grandmother used to say that good company makes good behavior.”

“Kelsie was always a follower,” Elspeth said. “And Janna was always the show-off.”

“She’s been doing at lot of that,” Voni said. “But in harmless ways. The other apprentices seem to find it entertaining rather than annoying.”

“Congratulations,” Marlys said.

“We wish we could take credit,” Elspeth said, “but the apprentices that Voni had before we came back seem to have the situation in hand.”

“That’s a credit to your training,” Voni said.

“You’re the one who spends the most time with the apprentices there,” Marlys said.

“Yes, but you trained me, and I trained the apprentices here the same way.”

“Then we can all take credit,” Marlys said. “I don’t doubt that Janna and Kelsie have never forgotten Elspeth’s watchful eye.”

“Oh, I make sure of that,” Elspeth said.

“Anything else?” Marlys said.

“Well, since we’re speaking of misbehavior,” Voni said, “how is it with you and Thorne?”

“No more difficult than I anticipated.”

"Good, but don't let your guard down around her," Elspeth said.

"I won't. I promise."

"Good night, then," Voni said, and they all exchanged farewells.

The next evening, as those on kitchen duty were beginning to clean up following supper, the image of a sorcerer appeared in the dining hall.

"Rochelle?" a sorcerer said.

"Here, Divira," Rochelle said. "Just finishing dinner."

"Sorry to interrupt," Divira said, "we have an emergency. We need sorcerers."

"What's the emergency?" Rochelle said.

A sound like nearby thunder reached their ears.

"What was that?" Rochelle said.

"That is the sound of a volcano exploding." Divira said. "The island sorcerers told us days ago it would erupt. Minutes ago, they told us it had erupted. Even though the volcano was below their horizon, they said the explosion was deafening at their location. They told us the sound would reach us in advance of the wave."

"Tsunami?" Rochelle said.

Divira nodded. "Worse than anything they ever saw. They said they were delayed in telling us because they were putting all their efforts into evacuation. It took every sorcerer they had, they said, to get everyone to high ground. Even though they went much higher than the markings of the worst tsunami they had heard of historically, they barely got out of the way of the water in time. They had to use sorcery to keep the edge away until the waters started to recede."

"So it's coming in your direction," Marlys said.

"Yes," Divira said, "We've already started evacuating people and animals. But you heard the sound...that means the wave is not far behind. Even shortening the distance, other sorcerers can't come to help in time. But your sorcerers, Fern and Bronwen, told us that you had powers from the Library of Sorcery to get here right away. We hope that you can."

"We'll come," Marlys said. "Just give us enough time to get organized."

"Thank you," Divira said, "I'd stay and confer with you, but we need every sorcerer we have here to continue the evacuation."

"Then don't delay," Marlys said. "We'll be there shortly."

Divira's image faded.

Thorne stood and looked around. "I've done flood control and evacuations before. I can lead this effort."

Marlys stood. "We're not leading evacuations. The sorcerers there can do that."

"What are you planning to do then, just light the way?" Thorne said.

Marlys took a deep breath. "When we were at the Library of Sorcery, the Head Librarian, Genevieve, told us that we were powerfully capable. We should be able to divert the surge."

"Impossible!" Thorne said. "Sorcery has its limits."

Serena spoke up. "Not impossible. We can do it. I read about a spell that can handle a tsunami while we were at the Library."

Tir turned to her with a grin. "I want to know more about that."

Serena stood. "If you follow me outside, I'll show you how to do it."

Everyone in the room followed her.

Once outdoors, Serena looked around. "Water is a fluid, like air. I can show you with leaves, when I can find a spot that still has them."

Rochelle pointed. "Over there."

They walked to the leaves. Serena found a drift and stood in front of it. "Watch." She started to gesture, casting a spell. "Pretend the leaves are the water. The water will first withdraw from the shore..." She pushed the leaves back. "...then surge forward." She pulled the leaves toward her. "When the waters are close to the beach, we fold the water coming forward underneath, like this." The leaves at the front dipped and moved back under the leaves coming forward. "As we do this, the water level will rise, but it will not reach the usual water's edge. Instead, it will pile up and we will see what seems to be a wall of water growing before us. As the surge expends itself, the waters will draw back and the water level will slowly lower until the ocean settles into its natural level."

"All right," Marlys said. "Tir, Rochelle, Nessa, Zaria, let's line up on either side of Serena and try it."

"Me?" Zaria said, "Do you mean me?"

Marlys smiled at her. "Yes, of course, I mean you."

"I can't do it," Zaria said.

Serena turned to her. "You have the power. You can do it."

"I haven't been a sorcerer for even a year yet."

"You have the power of the Library inside you," Tir pointed out. "Never doubt it."

Thorne waved at Zaria. "If the child says she can't do it, she can't do it."

Zaria glared at Thorne. She stood and faced Marlys. "I'll do my best, though I have no idea whether I can do this."

"Just try it," Marlys said.

Zaria walked to the end of the line. Astrid moved next to her.

Serena looked to the right and to the left. "Just start. The book said that when more than one sorcerer is doing this, the spell will coordinate a group effort."

Marlys took a deep breath and cast the spell. She could see the other five joining in. Astrid leaned over toward Zaria, speaking in a voice so softly that Marlys could not hear it, but it was clear that Astrid was coaching Zaria. Zaria nodded, and joined in.

Soon, they were all manipulating the leaves. They swirled in unison.

Serena put her arms down. "That is what we shall do."

The others rested and the leaves settled on the ground again.

"Ha!" Thorne said. "Do you think that just because you could move a few leaves in unison that you can direct an entire ocean?"

Marlys swung around and faced her. "Yes," she said firmly.

"Not an entire ocean," Rochelle said, "just enough to keep the water from flooding the six communities bordering the ocean." She looked around at the others. "We'll have to assemble on the mountain ridge overlooking the sea. The air can get cool there, so grab a jacket before we go."

Marlys nodded. "Do it quickly."

All six took off. Since the wedding, Marlys had been wearing her usual outfit: wide pants that seemed to act like a long skirt, a tailored shirt, sturdy shoes.

Thorne followed Marlys as she hurried to her room to get her jacket. "You can't really believe this will work."

"The Librarians wouldn't have recorded the spell if it didn't work. They had more experience than we had."

"Exactly. You've never even seen a tsunami before."

"There's always a first time."

Thorne snorted. She grabbed her own jacket when Marlys grabbed hers. "I'm going with you."

"You can watch," Marlys said, "but if you try to interfere…."

"I have no intention of doing so. I have to see what you're doing in order to undo any damage you cause from this reckless spell."

Marlys said no more, but put her jacket on while walking. She stopped in the dining hall where others had a gathered around a table holding a map of the Oceanside province.

Rochelle pointed to the communities marked on the map. "I'll be on the ridge overlooking Safe Harbor. Marlys, you take Challenger's Cove. Tir, you go here, Serena, here, Nessa, here, and Zaria, here."

Astrid put on a jacket. "I'll go with Zaria."

Marlys turned to Zaria. "Is this all right with you?"

Zaria nodded.

"Ridiculous," Thorne said. "Those points are leagues and leagues apart. How are you going to coordinate spells at those distances?"

Tir walked up to Thorne and leaned toward her ear. "Separately, and even more together, we are a powerful force."

Thorne snorted.

Marlys turned to the five others. "Everyone remember how to cast the traveling spell?" She saw nods and heard sounds of assent. "All right, let's go." She led the way out.

When Celestine saw Thorne follow Marlys, she said, "If Thorne is coming, I'm coming, too."

Thorne looked back. "I don't need a minder."

"You're getting one whether you need one or not." Celestine shrugged into a jacket.

"Do you want more of us to come with you?" Esme asked shyly.

"No," Marlys said gently. "I need the rest of you sorcerers and apprentices to remain here. We can't leave the fortress empty in case there's an emergency here while we're absent. Astrid, you're in charge while we're away."

She heard murmurings of assent in response.

Those going to the Oceanside region gathered outside and each cast the long-distance travel spell that Genevieve had taught them at the Library of Sorcery.

Once she had cast her spell, Marlys extended her arm toward opening and turned to Thorne. “You can step through first.”

“It’s a wonder that it’s possible to transport to such a great distance,” Thorne mumbled, and stepped through.

Marlys let Celestine go in front of her. Once at their destination, she found herself at the top of a ridge overlooking the ocean, standing next to Thorne and Celestine. She canceled the transportation spell and surveyed the area. People climbed the hills in their direction, but stopped at a plateau three-quarters of the way to Marlys’s location.

“The Oceanside sorcerers seem to have the matter in hand,” Thorne said. “The towns and farms below seem to be abandoned. The animals have also been driven up onto the hills.”

“True,” Marlys said. “But I still see stragglers being helped along...probably the old and infirm. And it is more than worth it to save the houses and farms. If the ocean destroys those, they would have to be rebuilt. The area might not recover completely for years.”

Thorne pointed westward. “The water is starting to draw back.”

Marlys nodded. As the ocean floor was revealed, it was possible to see old wreckage and debris, as well as rocks, shells, and other sea life. Lifting her head, she saw that the sun was lowering, though she did not yet have to shade her eyes against it.

“There are ships out there,” Thorne said.

“I know. I understand it’s better if they put out to sea ahead of the tsunami. The water away from shore is less fierce, and they won’t be dashed against the rocks on shore.”

“They may have problems, nonetheless,” Thorne said.

“I presume they are all experienced sailors and have seen worse,” Marlys said.

Thorne shook her head.

Surprisingly, two men ran out into the ocean, picking up newly revealed treasures on the sand.

“There are always fools,” Thorne said.

While Marlys wondered if she should act, she saw a sorcerer come out of a distance-shortening spell, grab the interlopers, and disappear again.

"I see that the local sorcerers are alert," Thorne said.

"They have done excellent work in evacuating everyone to higher ground," Marlys said.

"I only hope it's high enough," Thorne said. "The water has receded almost to the horizon. I have never seen a tsunami, but from all I've heard, that's bad news."

Glancing to the north, she saw a sorcerous light on a far distant ridge which was probably over Tir. To the south, just under the horizon, she could make out another light which Serena had probably kindled. She quickly placed a sorcerous orb overhead to mark her presence, and turned back to the ocean.

The surge came quickly. Marlys cast the spell and the water began folding under itself. How far would it go? She felt her spell merge with the others. The water rose in front of her, forming a wall. She extended the spell to the limit of her strength, hoping she, and the other five sorcerers, had the power to hold it.

Chapter 8

Slowly, the water level began to lower. While keeping her concentration, she sensed Thorne and Celestine casting spells around her. She did not have time, however, to determine what exactly they were doing.

When the water returned to its usual level, Marlys sighed and dropped the spell. She could feel the others dropping their spells also.

Celestine clapped Marlys on the shoulder. “You did it!”

Marlys smiled and glanced at Thorne, who shook her head.

Celestine pointed out to the ocean. The waters now lapped normally on the shore. “Thorne and I steadied the ships out at sea. It wasn’t much, compared to you....”

“It was well done,” Marlys said, “and necessary. I’m sure the sailors all appreciated it.”

“Nice of you to credit me with some value,” Thorne said.

“I always give credit where it is due,” Marlys said.

Thorne tossed her head.

“How did the others do, I wonder?” Celestine mused.

As if in answer, Tir appeared next to them.

“That was an experience,” he said. “I couldn’t see the rest of you except for your sorcerous beacons, but I could feel you adding your power to mine.”

Zaria and Astrid appeared next, giggling.

“Oh, that was fun!” Zaria said.

“You should have seen her,” Astrid added. “Folded the water, just as Serena said, and added a display to go with it. We took some of the surface water and had it dancing in the sky.”

“Down and back, down and back, until it stopped,” Zaria said. “Astrid gave me hints as I cast the spell.”

“That’s all I could give, hints,” Astrid said. “I assure you, I did not have the sorcerous strength to deal with a tsunami of that scale.”

The image of Rochelle appeared, as she contacted Marlys through the sorcerous channels. "All is well here. The High Sorcerer of Oceanside extends her thanks on behalf of the region."

"Please extend my greetings to her," Marlys said.

"I will. Our handling the tsunami freed the local sorcerers from vainly trying to protect the towns and farms from all that water, and concentrate their efforts on what they could do: get everyone to safety, steady ships at sea, that sort of thing. With your permission, I'll stay here for at least another few days. The islands experienced a flood far beyond historical proportions, and they have a lot of damage. I can get food and supplies there immediately, whereas it would take ships from here days to get there."

Marlys nodded. "Please stay as long as necessary. Do you require any help from the five of us?"

"No, I think I can handle it until they can supply and send ships."

"May the blessings of the Bright Beings remain on you then."

"And with you." Rochelle's image disappeared.

As Rochelle spoke, Serena, and then Nessa, appeared.

Serena turned to Thorne. "It is unwise to presume that a spell won't work unless you have seen it fail."

Thorne extended an arm toward the ocean. "No one living has ever seen anything like this! I think I can be pardoned for being skeptical."

Serena threw her an exasperated look.

"Time go to home," Marlys said.

When they emerged from the traveling spell, they found everyone at the fortress still outside, waiting.

"How did it go?" Esme asked.

Marlys smiled. "Success!"

The others cheered and applauded.

A thunderous sound drew their attention upward.

"Clear sky lightning?" Tir said.

"No, that's the sound of the volcano erupting finally reaching us. We're so far removed from Oceanside it took this long to travel the distance."

"That must have been a calamitous eruption, for the sound to have carried so far," Astrid said.

"I'm in the mood to go inside for tea and cakes," Celestine said. "Anyone care to join me?"

Everyone did.

Sunset outside found them all still in the dining hall. The sorcerers who stayed at the fortress were eager to hear of the experience of their colleagues. Thorne remained quiet, sipping her tea.

The image of Genevieve appeared in the dining hall.

Marlys faced it. "Genevieve."

"We have just realized that there was a catastrophic explosion in the mid-ocean. It will create a disastrous tsunami. It's too late to protect the islands, but there may be still time to save the coastline. Can you go quickly? You and your companions are the only sorcerers outside the Library district with the power to do so."

"We've been there and back," Marlys said. "We used a spell that Serena had read about at the Library to quell it."

"Thank the Universe," Genevieve said.

Marlys smiled. "The sorcerers on the islands were able to save the population there, though they experienced destruction. We prevented any damage to the coastal communities."

"Do the islands need sorcerous assistance?"

"We have addressed that, too," Marlys said.

"Then I ask your forgiveness for underestimating you," Genevieve said.

"No forgiveness is necessary," Marlys said. "It's better to give an unnecessary warning than none and face disaster."

Thorne stepped toward the image. "High Sorcerer Genevieve. I am High Sorcerer Thorne."

Genevieve's image faced her with a bland expression. "Yes?"

"As you just noted, there are only six sorcerers outside the Library with the power to deal with catastrophes. I wish to offer to come to the Library myself to increase those numbers."

The image of Genevieve turned to face Marlys. "I think it may interest you, Marlys, that since you left us, we had a convocation of sorcerers in the Library district. We agreed that you and the sorcerers accompanying you were worthy of the honor of being counted Librarians."

Marlys inclined her head. "Thank you."

"We considered ourselves fortunate that you and your companions, who managed to find us despite the spells at our borders, are all sorcerers of integrity. The sense of the convocation, however, was that we wished to prevent other sorcerers, who may not be as honorable, from breaching the sorcerous barriers. We felt that if you and your companions found a way, others would inevitably follow, perhaps in large numbers."

"I doubt it," Marlys said. "In the first place, reaching the Library district was extremely difficult and we nearly failed ourselves. Second, we all agreed that we would not tell anyone how we got there, and we have kept to that agreement."

"Nonetheless," Genevieve said, "the convocation agreed that we would put up additional barriers at our borders, and other sorcerers from the outside would not enter except at our invitation. This is not a judgment on the character of your sorcerers. We are confident that they are conducting themselves responsibly. But we are not comfortable letting anyone else in unless we know them well."

"You have the right to manage your district as you see fit," Marlys said. "We will respect that."

"You and your companions, of course, are welcome to return at any time." The image of Genevieve turned back to Thorne. "Your request is denied, for the reasons I have stated. As one who has served as a High Sorcerer, I am confident that you can serve your region well without benefit of a visit here."

Thorne stared at Genevieve's image in astonishment.

"Marlys," Genevieve said, "those sorcerers in my district more well read in natural disasters say we must be on the alert for other consequences of the volcanic eruption."

"Such as?" Marlys asked.

"Ash," Genevieve said.

"Can ash carry this far?" Marlys said.

"It can if it ascends to the upper reaches of the air surrounding this world. We have ancient records of ash blocking the sun for an entire year or longer."

"Are you certain this will happen?" Marlys asked.

"Certain, no. But it is a possibility we need to prepare for. We have sorcerers researching the problem and possible solutions. I may be contacting you again."

Marlys nodded. "And I you."

"Please do. Again, congratulations on your efforts with the tsunami."

"Thank you."

Genevieve's image faded.

Thorne silently turned and hurried out of the room.

The others gathered around Marlys.

Tir nodded in the direction Thorne had taken. "I wager she's not happy."

Celestine leaned toward Marlys. "May I confess how relieved I am? Since your return and Thorne's release, my greatest fear was that Thorne would find a way to the Library of Sorcery and increase her powers beyond what the rest of us could handle."

"We're still here," Nessa said.

"Yes, but that can't always be the case," Celestine said. "Your powers will be in demand, and what if all six of you are gone and tending to a disaster while we're here with Thorne? At least now, we're a match, especially working together."

Marlys saw nods from other sorcerers and apprentices.

"You're not disappointed that you may not be able to go to the Library of Sorcery and boost your powers, too?" Marlys said.

Astrid looked around at her colleagues. "I can't deny the thought occurred to me. It would be nice. But I have all the powers I need now, and it's certainly an enormous difference from when I was just working household spells."

Oriana, one of the apprentices, said, "I'd be happy to reach the level of Astrid, here, or Celestine."

Other apprentices made sounds of assent.

Marlys lingered a little longer in conversation with the others, then went to the kitchen and made up a tray. When she carried it out, Tir spotted her and said, "Two teacups?"

"Yes," Marlys said, "one for me and one for Thorne."

"It's commendable for you to think of her," Serena said, "but I don't think she'll be grateful for it."

"I know she won't," Marlys said. "But being kind takes little extra effort."

"I doubt that she will be won over by kindness," Tir said. "I wish she would, but I doubt she will."

Marlys inclined her head. "Nonetheless...."

When Marlys neared the suite, she heard voices and stopped. Although it occurred to her to turn back, she felt it would be irresponsible, again, not to hear what Thorne said to others. And, after all, she could see the door was open from her vantage point.

"They didn't want me, Elspeth," Thorne said.

"From what you told me, it wasn't just you, the Librarians didn't want anyone."

"I don't understand it. I am the High Sorcerer. My office was stolen from me, and no one seems to see the injustice in that. Instead, I am turned away as if I was the one who did wrong. No one here supports me."

"There are still those who feel affection toward you," Elspeth said, "I, for one, and others at other training centers."

"But I have to stay here. To leave would be seen as my agreeing that Marlys is High Sorcerer in Goldenvalley. I will not do that. There has to be some way to regain my office, and repay Marlys for her insolence."

"Have you thought of sharing the office? Voni and I are working together well, and I have reports of the same at other training centers."

"There's a difference between authority at a training center and authority over a region," Thorne said. "Besides, if I shared the office, that would be taken as a sign that I approved of what Marlys did, and that I will not do."

"You don't have to approve," Elspeth said. "You only have to work with her, for the good of the region. To most of the citizens here, you are a distant memory. I'm sorry to say so, but it is true. We must face that reality that twelve years have passed. It is a different world now."

"But not a better one," Thorne said bitterly.

"I think of it as carrying out our original vision, to improve and elevate the region."

Thorne snorted. "And then we found how cruel the world really is, and it must be met with force."

"Not always," Elspeth said. "They seem to have found a way around it, here."

"They will learn, as you and I did."

"If that's how you regard matters, then all you need to is to stand by and wait for their inevitable fall."

"That's precisely what I'm doing."

"You needn't feel alone, either. You've reached out to me. Reach out to the other sorcerers in our assembly. They may want to hear from you."

"Or they may not," Thorne complained. "They may already have been taken in, as you have."

"Taken in?" Elspeth protested.

"Sorry. I spoke out of turn. I know we are still friends. It's just that I feel so alone and isolated here."

"Then get out more. You told me you steadied the ships in the tsunami. You've demonstrated your worth. Demonstrate it in the region, as you used to do. People will respect that. Older ones will remember."

Marlys heard nothing for a few seconds.

"I will think on that." Thorne sounded reluctant, however.

"May the light of the Bright Beings shine on you."

"And on you."

Marlys waited a few moments after the conversation ended to enter the suite. She admired Elspeth's ability to maintain a precarious balance: keeping Thorne as a friend while trying to guide Thorne along another path. It must not be easy for her.

Certainly Thorne would not be inclined to listen to anyone at the Goldenvalley fortress. Marlys still found herself too distressed at what Thorne had done to her to try to help Thorne as Elspeth did. She wondered if Thorne would ever change her mind. Marlys strongly resolved not to let her guard down. Despite Marlys's greater powers, Thorne could still become a threat. Marlys would not let that happen.

Chapter 9

The next morning, Marlys awakened to the sound of raindrops pattering on her window. She got out of bed, walked over, and peered through the glass. After what Genevieve said, Marlys half-expected to see ash mixed in with the raindrops, but no, it was a typical autumn rain.

After visiting the lavatory and getting dressed, Marlys checked Thorne's room. She did not see Thorne there. The spell that would tell her if Thorne was nearby still was in force; Thorne was not nearby. But the locator spell variation put Thorne in the fortress's library. She must have had breakfast earlier and gone there afterward.

Marlys felt it was safe to leave Thorne where she was and go find her own breakfast. Looking through the windows of the dining hall, Marlys could see apprentices and sorcerers playing outside. Keeping oneself dry even in a pouring rain was a spell any sorcerer could cast, but the apprentices wore raincoats and hats. Nonetheless, they laughed and ran on the grounds, throwing handfuls of water at each other—a simple household spell that, gathering water in one's hands—and avoiding the water thrown by others.

Besides herself, only Tir and Serena sat at a table in the dining hall, sipping tea.

Marlys joined them. Celestine came out with a breakfast tray and placed it in front of Marlys, which she accepted with thanks.

"I presume Thorne was here earlier?" Marlys asked after swallowing a bite of bread.

"She ate breakfast here and then went to our library," Serena said. "We presume she's looking for spells that we've recorded since she was time-bound."

"That would include the spells you copied into our books after returning from the Library of Sorcery," Marlys said.

Serena nodded. "So far, I have only recorded spells I felt would be of general use. I read so many books it would take a lifetime to record all of the ones I found there."

"I trust your discretion," Marlys said.

"Of course, I'd tell you of any spells that we needed, as I did with the tsunami spell," Serena said. "You are right that there are some spells I'm not planning to record because they could be abused."

"Good thought," Tir said. "Thorne would certainly find a way to misuse them."

"Just about any spell could be misapplied," Marlys said.

"True," Serena said, "but some would have more dire consequences than others."

"I don't doubt it," Marlys said.

Thorne reappeared for the midday meal. By then sorcerers and apprentices had come back inside. They sat at a table by themselves, chatting merrily, while Marlys and her fellow Librarians sat together at another table. Thorne joined them, uninvited, taking an empty place.

"I read the climbing spell in our spell book," Thorne said as she set down the tray of food she had brought from the kitchen. "I recalled reading the same spell in one of the books along the Spell Passage. I was a first-year sorcerer then, eager, but not very experienced." She spread a napkin on her lap and reached for a breadroll. "I didn't think it was very important at the time. To tell the truth, I didn't think anything that I read or experienced would help me get past the boundaries of the Mountains of Wrath." She looked around at the others. "I suppose you found that spell useful in your quest?" She tore of a piece of bread, buttered it, and ate it, watching the others as she chewed.

Silence answered her.

After a few moments, Tir said, "Clever. Trying to catch us off-guard with friendly banter. Very smooth."

At the other end of the table, Zaria put her teacup down. "We said we weren't going to tell you how we got there."

Thorne swallowed and smiled. "But the High Sorcerer Librarian already said that they have barred entry with new spells. Surely it doesn't matter now."

Another pause.

Tir gestured toward Thorne with a fork. “You’re good.” He grinned at her.

Thorne attacked her piece of roast chicken with a knife and fork. “In any event, the spell seems to be sufficient to scale the walls here.” She threw Marlys a meaningful look.

“That’s true.” Serena gestured to the other table. “The sorcerers here entertained the apprentices by trying it out for an entire afternoon.”

“That’s what can happen if you write a spell into a book easily found in a library instead of on a piece of paper that’s rolled up and hidden in the walls,” Tir said.

“Some spells aren’t for the inexperienced and the unready,” Thorne said.

“Like the spells along the Spell Passage,” Tir said. “The inexperienced and the unready might completely discount them.” He leaned forward and stared at Thorne with a lifted eyebrow.

“That sounds familiar,” Nessa mumbled.

Thorne turned to Nessa once, then twice, as if trying to determine whether the remark was meant for her or someone else. Then she returned her attention to her food.

They finished the meal without further conversation. Nessa and Zaria finished first and brought their plates to the kitchen before walking to the common rooms. When Thorne was done, she stood, started to walk to the back exit, and then turned and took her tray back to the kitchen before leaving the dining hall.

“She may be learning,” Tir said.

“More likely trying to lull us into inattention before springing a surprise,” Serena said. “I don’t think she’ll be much daunted by Tir calling her on it.”

Marlys nodded. “I would expect her to test us at any opportunity. I’m glad that Nessa and Zaria are also alert to it.”

“They were the ones who first proposed that we all agree never to tell anyone,” Serena said. “That tells us that this is an issue of great importance to them.”

“No less to us,” Marlys said.

Rochelle returned from Oceanside after the evening meal. Marlys and Thorne had retired to their respective rooms by then,

Marlys to keep the daily record and Thorne writing who-knew-what in her journal. At least it was quiet except for the sound of quills scratching on paper, Marlys thought.

"Rochelle's back!" echoed through the fortress...apprentices calling to each other.

Marlys put her quill and the book away, secured her room, and walked past Thorne—who did not look up—to the door of the suite and then out to the hallway.

She found Rochelle in the dining hall, surrounded by sorcerers and apprentices.

"Have you had dinner yet?" Celestine asked.

"No, I haven't," Rochelle said.

"Sit, then," Astrid said, "we'll bring you something."

"Thank you." Rochelle lowered herself into a seat with a sigh.

The others drew back when Marlys approached. The result was that Marlys could sit next to Rochelle. "Hard work?" she said, as others took places around them.

Rochelle nodded.

Marlys put a hand to Rochelle's hairline. "Is that ash?"

Rochelle reached up and brushed it off, checking her hand when she brought it down. "Yes. I thought I'd got it all, but there was so much of it." She whisked the remainder of it away by sorcery.

"How are things on the islands?" Marlys asked.

"Covered with ash," Rochelle said. "Or, at least, it was. We had a team of sorcerers working for hours to clear it away. Most of it is gone, now. At least enough to set up temporary shelters for people and animals."

"Any casualties?" Marlys asked.

"The Bright Beings truly smiled on us," Rochelle said. "Nothing beyond a few bumps and bruises from people in a hurry to get away from the rising waters."

Astrid came in with a tray and set it in front of Rochelle.

"We can sit here quietly while you eat," Marlys said.

Rochelle grasped a teacup. "No need, if you don't mind me pausing for food and drink."

"Not at all." Marlys saw movement out of the corner of her eye and turned to see Thorne come in. She sat at a far table, well within the range of hearing, facing them with hands in her lap.

After Rochelle had consumed a few pieces of bread and some sweetberries, Marlys asked, "Do you think they will need any further assistance from us?"

Rochelle swallowed a bite of chicken. "No. Our saving Oceanside meant that no rebuilding had to be done there, and they were free to supply the islands in their need. We brought in enough food and other supplies to last until ships from the coast could reach them with more. The sorcerers on the islands were able to save most of their fishing fleet, so they will be able to quickly provide food for themselves, and we managed to clear ash from their springs and wells."

"Good work," Marlys said.

Rochelle shrugged. "Most of I did was to provide transport, though I did my share of clearing ash as well."

"That transport was something no other sorcerer there could have provided."

Rochelle nodded. "True. The island sorcerers wanted to add their thanks."

Marlys smiled. "We shall consider ourselves appreciated, then." She and the others waited while Rochelle finished her roast chicken slices. "Genevieve contacted us through the sorcerous channels while you were away."

Rochelle turned to Marlys. "She did?" Rochelle said eagerly. "What did she say?"

"First, we're honorary Librarians...that is, the six of us who were there."

"I'll take it."

"However, they've cast additional spells to be sure no one else comes in from outside except at their express invitation."

"That does not surprise me."

"Further, she said that we would have to prepare to deal with ash here."

Rochelle considered. "I didn't see any sign of it spreading."

Marlys pointed upward. "In the far reaches of the sky. She said they have records of the distant past in which the sun was obscured for a year because of ash from a volcano."

Rochelle inhaled and nodded slowly. "Oh, yes. There were stories, stories I was told when I was young. As you say, it was a very long time ago, if it really happened."

"They think it really happened," Marlys said. "They have sorcerers studying possible remedies in case it happens here."

"I don't know if there is enough sorcery to provide for the entire continent if we don't have any sun," Rochelle said.

"Obviously they found a way to survive even then," Marlys said. "Else we wouldn't be here today."

"True, but was there a famine? And were there casualties?" Rochelle said. "The stories I heard mentioned a famine and great suffering."

"That we will try to avoid," Marlys said. "But for now, everything's fine, and we may not have to deal with such a disaster at all."

"I certainly hope so," Rochelle said.

Chapter 10

The next morning, Marlys awoke to sunshine streaming through her windows, casting bright squares on the wooden floor. She rose, washed, dressed, and left the suite. Instead of going straight to the kitchen or dining hall, she walked downstairs, out the front door and looked up. She saw nothing but a brilliant blue sky unobscured by even wispy clouds.

"I've been looking, too," Tir said.

Marlys turned to see Tir standing at her right. "Let's hope the sky stays clear."

They walked inside together.

At most of the meals, the apprentices sat together at the far end of a table, followed by the sorcerers, followed by Marlys, Tir, Serena, and Rochelle. This was not enforced by any rule, it simply happened that way. Marlys was satisfied letting anyone sit where they wanted to, and occasionally there was no particular order at all.

Thorne sometimes took a place near everyone else, and other times, she sat alone. This particular morning, she sat alone at the next table over, across from Marlys. She was close enough to hear the conversation and add to it if she wished.

As those on kitchen duty cleared the tables, Celestine and one of the apprentices, Lyra, approached Marlys. Marlys stayed seated, but turned to Celestine and Lyra, who clearly wished to speak to her.

"Lyra believes she's ready to awaken her sorcery," Celestine said. "As you know, she's worked hard, even in your absence, and I know she will make a great sorcerer."

Marlys smiled and turned to Lyra. "I agree. We can set up a crucible for her to break through."

Lyra bowed her head, not making eye contact, but faced in Marlys's direction. "There's something I haven't said before. I'm afraid of enclosed places. I panic if I'm shut up in a closet. Is there another way?"

"A true sorcerer overcomes fear," Thorne interjected.

Tir turned around to face Thorne. "And what of your fears?"

Thorne scoffed. "I have no such fears."

"On the contrary," Tir said, "you do. You are afraid of losing your standing in the sorcerous community. You are afraid of losing the respect of your peers. You are afraid that you will be perceived as valueless, useless. Only when you overcome those fears will your life have any meaning."

Marlys watched Thorne's face closely. She looked stunned.

The entire room fell silent for a few moments.

Thorne stood and glared at Tir. "You know nothing." She stalked toward the rear doorway, bumping into a table as she went. She quickly regained her footing and hurried out.

"You rattled her," Rochelle said.

"Where did you get that kind of insight?" Celestine said. "Not that you didn't have insight before, but...."

Tir leaned toward Marlys. "I remembered all the lectures Marlys gave us as to how to handle deceivers we might encounter in the course of our sorcerous work."

"It's more than that," Serena said.

Tir nodded. "At the Library of Sorcery, I studied books about the sorcerous wars. The sorcerers then felt that more than spells were needed to defeat their opponents. They wanted to know the reasons behind aggression and how to counter that. Their conclusion was that a lot of aggression originated in fear. They wrote entire books about it."

Celestine turned to Marlys. "It really is unfortunate that more cannot access the Library. Not necessarily to make our sorcery stronger, but to gain from the wisdom they accumulated."

"Agreed," Serena said. "But still, in the wrong hands, such knowledge could be used to turn us against each other."

"I suppose so," Celestine said.

Marlys addressed Lyra again. "The sorcerers at the Library of Sorcery told us that they simply find a task beyond the ability of the apprentice. We'll work on it and find one for you."

"I know," Lyra said, "but I'm the oldest of the apprentices now. I'm as old as Tir, and he's been a sorcerer for three years."

Tir moved over, and still seated, took Lyra's hands in his and smiled. "Look at me, Lyra."

Lyra did so.

"We all know how hard you work. You've refined your household spells and even found new uses for them. You will become a great sorcerer. Not all of us can become a sorcerer in a month, like Celestine did. I know it's hard to be patient when you see other apprentices becoming sorcerers. But you'll get there."

"What we don't want you to do," Marlys added, and Lyra turned to her, "is do something desperate to become a sorcerer. We met a sorcerer along the spell passage who had part of her foot cut off. We don't want you to do something like that."

"Universe forbid!" Zaria called from where she sat. "Lyra, we don't know each other well, but I tried to do something desperate along the way to the Library of Sorcery. Marlys and Nessa saved me, or else I might have died. But a challenge came later, one I didn't foresee, and I knew in my heart and soul that this was the time. I became a sorcerer."

Marlys looked from Zaria to Lyra. "Lyra, none of us need to go out searching for adversity, as happened when Thorne was High Sorcerer and before. Adversity will come on its own. I fell into a clutching bog one day, completely by accident. When something like that happens, you will know it is time. You will rise to the challenge and meet it. Your sorcery will awaken."

Serena leaned toward Lyra. "Lyra, I read many more spells than I could possibly write down if I wrote for the rest of my life. Thorne may be wrong about many things, but she's not wrong in that some spells are only for the mature. Let me teach you some of those spells. You're ready for them. Then, when your sorcery does awaken, and it will, you will have a wealth of magical knowledge to call upon."

"How does that sound?" Marlys asked.

Lyra smiled and nodded. "Yes. Thank you!"

Marlys stood and patted Lyra's arm. "You'll do well. We all know it."

In the years since she wrapped Thorne and the others in a time-bind, Marlys instructed and trained apprentices, at first by herself. Then, as the years went by, those she trained were able to train others. She still spent a significant amount of time with the apprentices and less experienced sorcerers, but she also shared in sorcerous tasks and administrative duties. This particular morning, she talked to the apprentices about their experiences when they accompanied other sorcerers and observed how they accomplished their tasks. The instruction included not only how to cast spells and which spells to cast, but also how to deal with stubborn or angry people. These skills, too, were necessary for their success.

As she talked to the apprentices, her locator spell told her that Thorne was walking through the fortress, especially the lower levels. When she dismissed the apprentices to their other assigned duties—cooking, cleaning, gardening, attending to animals—Marlys went to see what all the wandering was about.

As she reached one of the staircases to the lower levels, she met Rochelle.

"I see you are wondering as much as I am what Thorne might be up to," she said.

"Searching for hidden spells, I think," Marlys said.

Rochelle nodded. "One would think that by now, with all the searches we have done, we would have found them all. But there always seems to be a crevice we've overlooked."

"Or one guarded by a spell that kept anyone from seeing the hiding place without effort," Marlys said.

They had not gone far, walking through the lower corridors, when they heard a cry and a thud. Marlys and Rochelle hurried to an open door at the top of a set of stairs. The room below was lit with dim sorcerous light, enough for them to see Thorne lying still at the bottom.

Marlys kindled a brighter sorcerous light and scrambled down the stairs, Rochelle right behind her. She knelt next to Thorne, who was lying on her back, eyes closed, but breathing. Marlys put a hand on Thorne's shoulder and sorcerously evaluated her condition.

She looked up briefly at Rochelle. "Head injury. I'll heal it."

"I'll stand by."

Marlys nodded and worked the healing spell.

Thorne inhaled deeply and opened her eyes. She lifted herself on her elbows and turned from Marlys to Rochelle. "Knocked the breath out of me," she said, and struggled to her feet. Marlys exchanged a knowing glance with Rochelle and assisted.

Thorne gently pulled free of Marlys's grasp. "I can go on from here."

"Perhaps it may be good to rest for awhile," Marlys suggested.

Thorne's face began to compose itself into a scowl but quickly reorganized into a neutral expression. "I'll just take a stroll." She walked up the stairs, slowly, as Marlys and Rochelle watched from the bottom.

Once Thorne was out the door, and her footsteps died away, Marlys said, "She's out of earshot."

"Not even a thanks, not that I expected any," Rochelle said.

"I didn't, either," Marlys said, and canceled the sorcerous light. The room dimmed, illuminated only by the ongoing glow.

"Wind knocked out of her indeed," Rochelle said.

"If that's what she wants to believe, it does no harm to let her," Marlys said. "She wouldn't acknowledge anything more dire, because that would be admitting that we are in the stronger position."

"How long do we have to humor her?" Rochelle asked.

"As much or as little as we want," Marlys said.

Rochelle faced Marlys squarely. "You know, we could have just left her and let nature take its course. That would have resolved the problem. The injury was serious enough so that we would not have to deal with her anymore. If she hadn't died, her brain would have been wrecked and she would have had little power."

"That goes against my principles," Marlys said. "Besides, I found out after I cast the time-bind twelve years ago that what you think resolves a problem could only create new ones."

"True," Rochelle said, "I was only speaking an idea that occurred to me. If I had come across her alone, I would have done the same as you."

Marlys nodded. "I know. It's done more than most know. My magistrate father and grandmother told me of cases when a scoundrel had a serious accident and the neighbors simply didn't summon a healer or sorcerer. If father or grandmother found such a case, they always lectured the community against it, since if the victim healed in spite of it all—and it did happen—that person would be angrier than ever. Besides, summoning a magistrate is how our world wants to deal with misdeeds. Civil order depends on it. My father said that dealing with outlaws by being outlaws only makes more outlaws."

“It does happen nonetheless, as you say,” Rochelle said. “In Oceanside, we call it throwing someone overboard. I heard stories of getting a miscreant drunk, rowing them out well into the ocean, and dropping the rogue over the side. I don’t know how much credit to give such stories, but I heard them.”

“That’s the reason I do my best to teach helpfulness even to the undeserving, so that it doesn’t happen here,” Marlys said.

Chapter 11

Later that day, Marlys received a sorcerous communication from Voni and Elspeth.

"May I ask if you're alone?" Voni said.

"Yes. I'm in the audience hall," Marlys said. "No one else is near."

"You remember Caleb, don't you?" Voni asked.

Marlys smiled. "Of course. I helped establish his farmstead after he married."

"Speaking of which," Voni said, "his wife, Jessie, recently gave birth to a child, Roxy. The midwives did their work well and had gone the day before we visited. I performed the usual after delivery healing."

"Thank you for that. I'm sure Jessie appreciated it."

"She did," Voni said.

"That isn't what we came there for, though," Elspeth added. "We were there to help bring the harvest in and ask to take a sorcerer's share."

"Was there any trouble?" Marlys said. "Caleb has always been generous to us."

Elspeth and Voni turned to each other, and then back to Marlys.

"The harvest went well," Elspeth said. "We gathered all the grain and put it in the barns. Caleb was with Voni the entire time I was working the spell and directing the apprentices. Once the task was complete, Caleb turned to thank us, and he recognized me, Janna, and Kelsie."

"Good memory. The last time he saw you, he was a child."

Elspeth nodded.

"He became very angry," Voni said. "He told me that you had promised him that Thorne and her helpers would never bother him again. He ordered us to leave his property at once and never come back. We left speedily without taking a sorcerer's share."

"When we got back to the training center," Elspeth said, "I had to explain to Janna and Kelsie that no, we could not have simply taken our share without his consent, and yes, we had to leave when he told us to."

"Sorcerers have respected a citizen's right for centuries," Marlys said. "I'm surprised Janna and Kelsie didn't know this."

"Probably my fault for assuming everyone on the continent grew up knowing this," Elspeth said.

"We can get along without our sorcerer's share," Voni said. "Our own garden produced abundantly this year, and our animals are thriving. But I feel sorry that he had the impression that I misled him."

"Not you. Me." Marlys said. "I'll go talk to him."

"It's a long way from the fortress," Elspeth said, then added quickly, "Oh, I forgot. The transportation spell you learned at the Library can carry you farther and faster than merely shortening distances."

"Can you leave Thorne alone?" Voni said.

"She won't be alone," Marlys said. "She's been searching the fortress for hidden spells. Right now, Tir and Rochelle are shadowing her. Besides those two, Serena, Nessa, and Zaria are here at present if they need help. I don't think they will, though. Thorne fell down a flight of stairs in the lower levels and I had to heal an otherwise deadly head injury. She won't be at her full strength for a while."

"Do you mind if I make a brief visit?" Elspeth said. "She might find my presence calming."

"You can come if you wish, though please wait until after I return after talking to Caleb."

"Just use the sorcerous channels when ready," Elspeth said.

"I will," Marlys said.

"There's one more thing," Elspeth added. "Caleb isn't the only one who's been uneasy. Filix spied Janna and Kelsie when they came into town with other apprentices for shopping. He asked us if there was going to be a return to the older ways."

"We assured him this would not happen," Voni said. "But other training centers have contacted us sorcerously and told us that citizens around them have noticed members of your old assembly walking around and have asked questions, too."

"Or acted worried," Elspeth added.

"None of them contacted me," Marlys said.

"They said didn't want to bother you unnecessarily when they knew that you had your hands full with Thorne," Elspeth said.

"Besides," Voni said, "you've told us that we're wise enough to act independently and only need to approach you if the issue is serious."

"I think this is serious enough," Marlys said.

"At present," Elspeth said, "they were just asking us what we were doing and if we noticed the same."

"Some of them are disguising themselves, using masking spells," Voni said. "So far, there's no sign of panic, just caution. Celeb has been the only case I know of real anger."

"I see," Marlys said. "Thank you for telling me."

When Elspeth's and Voni's images faded away, Marlys found Serena and Celestine using the near-distance locator spell. They were with Lyra, tutoring her on various spells.

"Sorry to interrupt," Marlys said. "I need to leave for a brief time to talk to Celeb."

"Anything wrong?" Celestine asked.

"Voni reported that he became angry when he saw Elspeth, Janna, and Kelsie," Marlys said. "He was afraid that we were going back to the old ways."

"Never," Serena said.

"Not while I have breath in my body," Celestine said.

"I need to go and reassure him," Marlys said. "Tir and Rochelle are shadowing Thorne, who's been resting in the sitting room. I don't think she'll cause any trouble while I'm gone, but I thought I'd let you know in case anything happens."

"We'll take over for you," Celestine said.

Marlys nodded. "I know I can count on all of you."

Marlys appeared on Celeb's farmstead in the wide space between the house and barn. Looking around, she did not see Celeb or Jessie, so she knocked at the door.

"Come in," Jessie called.

Marlys entered. Only Jessie stood in the main room, next to a cradle.

Before Marlys could say anything, Jessie smiled and walked toward her. "Marlys. Good to see you again."

"It's good to see you too, Jessie." They clasped hands briefly.

"Can I get you something?" Jesse asked. "I have a plate of sliced pears on the table."

"I'll be happy to take a slice, thanks." Marlys put reached for one and ate it. "Delicious. Thank you." She nodded toward the cradle. "I understand you and Caleb have a baby."

"Come see." She walked over to the cradle.

Marlys looked down to see the baby, sleeping peacefully.

"Congratulations," she said softly.

Jessie nodded. "We're so happy."

Marlys straightened up and faced her. "I wanted to talk to Caleb. Is he around?"

Jessie's expression sobered. "He's in the barn. He's angry. Sorcerers came earlier today and helped us with the harvest. Some of the sorcerers, he said, were the ones who witnessed him being beaten as a child. He ordered them to go away. He didn't mean anything by it," she finished quickly.

"No one took offense," Marlys said, noticing that Jessie looked relieved. "I just wanted to explain." She put a reassuring hand on Jessie's arm. "No one's going to come and hurt you. I give you my word."

Jessie nodded. "He's in the barn. You can go talk to him. I have to stay with the baby."

"Of course. Congratulations again." Not wanting to leave without some sort of blessing, she bent down over the child's cradle. "Sleep well, little one. May the blessings of the Bright Beings stay with you." She looked up at Jessie.

Jessie gasped and put a hand up to cover her mouth.

"Is something wrong?" Marlys asked.

"No…no. It's just that…you're glowing."

"Oh." Marlys put a hand up to her hair, wondering if she ought to look into a mirror. "I've been to the Library of Sorcery. The magic there does that to a sorcerer."

"Does it make you more powerful?"

Marlys smiled. "It does. You have nothing to fear, though."

Jessie shook her head. "I'm not afraid. Especially if you're more powerful now. I know you will protect us."

"I will. I promise."

There was a mirror in the house. Marlys checked herself before going out and saw the aura, of course. Perhaps a hint of an additional glow that was now fading, then gone. She smiled and nodded again at Jessie and walked out.

The barn door was open. Marlys saw Caleb sitting on a crate, head bowed.

"Caleb?" Marlys ventured.

Caleb looked up and ran a hand through his hair. "I'm sorry. I didn't mean anything. I don't know what came over me."

Marlys waved a reassuring hand. "You don't need to apologize." Looking around, she grabbed another crate and sat opposite Caleb. "I was there, too, and I got slapped by Thorne for protesting."

Celeb shook his head. "I'll never understand it. They came and said there was a deed signing, and if I came, I and my family would get food. Of course, my parents thought it was a great honor and sent me with the landowners. I watched the signing ceremony and then I and the other boys there were beaten. When I asked why, they said it was because I was a witness. It was so I would remember." He looked Marlys in the eye. "I didn't need to be beaten to remember."

Marlys nodded. "That's the reason children are given special badges now instead of a beating. They remember just as well."

"Seeing those sorcerers, the apprentices, the ones who were there, too, just brought it all back."

Marlys reached out and touched Caleb's arm. "I'm so sorry."

"I couldn't walk well for a year afterwards. If it wasn't for one of those wandering sorcerers from the south coming through town and healing me, I still would have trouble walking."

Marlys drew her hand back. "I hadn't heard of that part of the story before. I didn't see you between the time of the deed signing and the time I was able to come back as High Sorcerer, when I helped you and your family and the other needy families in town repair your houses and get some decent work."

"I didn't bring it up because I didn't want you to think I was ungrateful."

"I would not have thought that. Please believe me."

Caleb nodded. "I do. But Jessie and I, we've just had a child, and I couldn't bear the thought of someone taking our child for a beating."

"That will not happen. I promise," Marlys said firmly. "I will not lie to you. Thorne is back. The old assembly is back. But things are different now. I and the other sorcerers you have known in recent years will not allow any going back to the old ways. We're wiser now, and more powerful in word if not in deed."

Caleb sighed.

Marlys gave him time to collect his thoughts.

After a while, Caleb gestured around the barn. "You can take your sorcerer's share. I have more than enough."

Marlys considered. If the volcano ash was going to spread, if it was going to cover the sky and block the sun, everyone would need to have reserves to draw upon. "Keep it for now. If we need it, we'll come for it. I will remember your offer, and thank you."

When Marlys returned to the fortress, she ascertained that Thorne had not moved from the sitting room. Tir and Rochelle kept out of her line of sight, but would know if Thorne was in any distress. Was Thorne resting? Thinking? Plotting?

I'll know soon enough, Marlys thought.

Chapter 12

Whether the sky was cloudy or clear, Marlys rose at about the same time every day. This day when Marlys opened her eyes, she saw an overcast sky outside.

When she reached the dining hall, she saw some of the apprentices and sorcerers standing at the windows. They turned when Marlys approached them.

Oriana turned to her. "Is this the volcano ash in the sky we heard was coming?"

"It may be," Marlys said. "Let me take a look."

Outside, more sorcerers and apprentices had gathered together, talking in low tones, scanning the horizon.

Marlys turned around. Whatever was in the air, from the horizon to high above her, appeared to be clouds: light gray in places, dark gray in others. Enough daylight had penetrated, now that the obscured sun had risen higher, that this could have been simply another cloudy day. Except that the clouds seemed extraordinarily high in the sky.

Serena turned to her. "What do you think?"

"Right now, I don't know," Marlys said. "Let's go in and have breakfast. Once we've eaten, I'll open a sorcerous channel to the Library of Sorcery and see if they know anything." With gestures, she herded everyone back inside.

During the meal, Thorne sat by herself, placidly buttering her bread and sipping her tea while those at the other tables spoke in subdued tones.

As they were cleaning up, Genevieve's image appeared in the room. "Marlys?"

"Here." Marlys was already standing, about to take her tray back to the kitchen. Astrid quickly stepped over and took it from her so she could devote her full attention to the conversation.

"The sun didn't appear here today," Genevieve said, "so I presume it didn't appear there, either."

"No," Marlys said. "The clouds seem stationed unusually high."

Genevieve nodded. "That's the ash. The ash has been spreading throughout the atmosphere ever since the day of the eruption. The skywatchers among us have noticed this. Most, including me, haven't noticed the ash because it wasn't yet thick enough to obscure sunlight to any great degree."

"Now it has," Marlys said.

"The skywatchers believe that we won't see the sun again for quite some time," Genevieve said.

Marlys heard soft gasps among those around her. "How long?"

"That depends on how long it takes for us to disperse it," Genevieve said.

"So we can disperse it," Marlys said hopefully.

"Our historical records seem to say so," Genevieve said, "but it will not be easy and it will not be fast."

"Do you have a plan?" Marlys said.

"We're working on one," Genevieve said. "The skywatcher sorcerers are discussing which spells might work best. We know what has been used in the past, but we have other spells, perhaps better spells, now."

"What can we do to help?" Marlys asked.

"For the ash, there's nothing you need to do now," Genevieve said. "Nothing drastic will happen for months. Since it is autumn, it doesn't matter whether plants can grow. The winter will be harsh, however, as the ash will block the sun's heat."

"You expect that this will be with us through winter?" Marlys asked.

"Yes. The general population needs to be informed, but we're going to share the news at a moderate pace, and you can, too. To everyone else, it will, at first, seem as if this is just a usual stretch of cloudy days. After a month, though, everyone is going to get tired of seeing dreary days."

Tir raised a hand and waved it. "I learned your spell of lighting the sky. That should provide some relief."

Genevieve nodded. "We're planning to use that here, too. That spell covers a large area, perhaps as large as one of your regions, but to cover most of the continent, you'll have to spread out. We're planning to send Librarians into your area to help with the work. Can you inform other regions, telling them what to expect?"

Marlys nodded. "We can get started on that task right away."

Serena stepped closer to the image. "Do you need me to come and read more spell books?"

"We'll remember your offer," Genevieve said, "but we think we have all the spells we need at the moment. Since you taught Blair the speed reading spell, he's been going through the Library to see whether there's anything additional we can use. However, we may call upon you in the future at need. No one else here can work your speed reading spell. It makes the rest of us dizzy."

Serena chuckled and nodded. "I know. That's the reason I'm the only one who can use it here."

"We'll keep you up to date on our progress," Genevieve said, "but that's all I have for you now."

"Thank you," Marlys said.

Genevieve's image disappeared.

The other sorcerers and apprentices gathered around Marlys.

"What's next?" Celestine asked.

"We'll have to contact all the sorcerers in the regions we can," Marlys said.

"Would it be helpful if I got out a map?" Astrid said.

Marlys nodded and Astrid ran out.

"Did I hear Genevieve say 'he?'" Celestine asked with a smile.

"Yes!" Tir said. "There's a senior Librarian in their district who's a man, and we also met a senior sorcerer along the Spell Passage who's a man."

Marlys saw Thorne, at the edge of the crowd, sigh and shake her head.

Celestine spied Thorne, too, and turned back to Tir. "Nice to have company!"

"I agree completely," Tir said.

Rochelle stepped up. "I'm concerned about the islands. They're out in the middle of the ocean, and won't be affected by lighting spells on the continent. In addition, they're the ones suffering the most."

"Since an island has a smaller area," Tir said, "our sorcerous beacon spell should serve to provide more light when needed."

"I've modified one of the household spells," Lyra said. "It spreads light a little more than a usual household lighting spell, enough to cover the area of a cottage or barn. It's not much, but...." She shrugged.

Marlys reached over and put a hand on Lyra's shoulder. "It could light an entire town, house-to-house. Not an insignificant spell by any means."

Lyra smiled.

Astrid ran in with a large, rolled-up map and spread it over a table. "Here's our map of the entire continent."

Thorne stepped up and fingered a corner. "It's so old it's needed sorcery to preserve it."

"It'll do for now," Marlys said.

"I would expect either the Spell Passage or the Library of Sorcery to have better maps," Serena said. "Some parts of the continent are not well defined on this map. While the shores of the continent are well marked, there are large blank areas which were unknown to us before our journey to the Library."

Everyone gathered around the table with the map. For a time, the room remained silent.

Rochelle looked up. "At least there isn't another continent on this world that we need to be concerned about."

"Is there?" Oriana asked. "Has anyone checked?"

"Yes," several voices said at once.

"The entire world has been charted my mariners," Marlys said. "They've sailed around the whole continent, through the north and south poles, and from the western shores around the globe to the eastern shores."

"The islands have all been charted as well," Rochelle said.

"The problem is with the distant territories," Thorne said. "There's minimal governance there, small and scattered populations, and little commerce between them and us."

Marlys nodded. "Here's what we know from our journey. There is a northern forest area, beyond the Library district, which is bordered by the Mountains of Wrath." She used a finger to trace the borders on the blank areas. "Then there are the eastern coastlands, mostly grassland. The parts we're familiar with are the southeastern mining areas and the southern regions extending north to the Spell Passage.

The remainder of the continent is our area, divided into our sorcerous regions."

"I presume we aren't going to ignore the northern and eastern borderlands," Tir said.

"Genevieve will probably send Librarians there," Marlys said. "The sorcerous community in the Library district is large enough to spare a couple of sorcerers to make sure they're not neglected. If she doesn't, and I can't imagine she won't, we can find a way to help them."

"We have only six Librarians here, and you will all be needed for our regions," Thorne said.

Marlys turned to her. "There are over 70 Librarians. Those numbers will be more than sufficient to cover the Library district and send a couple of dozen here to reinforce our strength."

"The immediate need is for communication," Serena said. "We have to alert all the sorcerers in all of our regions, plus the southern Ambassadors, plus the Spell Passage. They, in turn, will have to inform the citizens in their areas what to expect this winter."

Marlys looked around. "Shall we assign each of the sorcerers here a region to contact?"

Nessa held up both hands and waved. "I read the spell that can help us there."

Everyone turned to her.

"The spell I memorized can reach a number of sorcerers at once," Nessa said. "There's no need to use the regular sorcerous channels, where those at one location can only speak to those at one other location."

Marlys turned to Nessa. "Excellent. Do you wish to speak to them or would you prefer that I write down for you the information we need to cover."

Nessa shook her head. "Like the sorcerous channel, anyone close to the origin or end point can see and hear. But you still need to know a sorcerer at the destination to make contact. I can show you how to do it, and then you can cast the spell."

"Thank you," Marlys said.

"Did you write this in the spell book?" Serena asked.

"No, I haven't yet," Nessa said.

"Can you wait until I can get the spell book to write it down?" Serena said.

"I'll go get it," Oriana said, and ran.

"Yes, I can wait." Nessa said.

"I'll go grab pen and ink," Astrid said, and hurried away.

Once in possession of the materials, Serena sat and wrote while Nessa explained the spell to Marlys. All the other apprentices and sorcerers gathered around and listened silently, breathlessly. Marlys saw Thorne out of the corner of her eye paying particular attention, positioning herself just behind Serena and looking over Serena's shoulder as she wrote. Marlys felt a communication spell was harmless enough for Thorne to learn, and besides, it seemed that only a Librarian had the strength to cast it anyway.

When Nessa finished, Marlys stepped back. The others cleared a space for her, and Marlys cast the spell.

"Fellow sorcerers," she began. "This is Marlys of Goldenvalley. I have an important announcement for you all."

"Are you contacting more than one of us?" Gweneth asked from Castlemount.

"Yes, I am," Marlys said. "This is a Library of Sorcery spell."

"You made it! Congratulations!" Clea said from Landsmere.

"While at the Library, those of us who came there found that our sorcerous strength increased," Marlys said. "We'll need all of that and more to bring us through the coming crisis."

"What crisis is that?" Lindra asked.

"A volcano exploded in the middle of the ocean," Marlys said. "It was an eruption of historic proportions. Besides creating a tsunami, which we thwarted sorcerously, it has spread ash in the skies throughout the globe. All of you have must have noticed that the sky is overcast."

"Everywhere?" Durand asked.

"Everywhere," Marlys confirmed. "We will not see the sun again for weeks, if not months." She paused for a few moments to let that sink in.

"The Librarians tell us," Marlys continued, "that there are spells that can dispel the ash."

"Won't it dispel by itself?" Ware asked.

"They say that may take over a year," Marlys said.

"A year! We can't be without sun for year," Lindra said. "The crops will fail."

"Exactly why they are working on a plan to dispel the ash," Marlys said.

"Are they going to teach us the spells?" Ilse asked.

"I'm guessing it will take the strength of a Librarian to work the spells," Marlys said. "There are six of us here in Goldenvalley with that level of strength, and the Library of Sorcery will send their Librarians throughout the regions to help."

"Why not let us go there and increase our strength?" Ilse asked.

"Still wary from the sorcerous wars would be my guess," Durand said.

"You're right, Durand," Marlys said. "We were a surprise. After we left, they reinforced their borders so no one else can come in without their invitation. I hasten to add that there are more than enough sorcerers in the Library district to spread throughout the continent."

"I don't think it's responsible for us to sit here, do nothing, and let them do all the work," Lindra said.

"That's the main reason I'm contacting you," Marlys said. "You'll need to inform the citizens in your area to prepare for a harsh winter. We have used spells for years to help with that."

Tir stepped forward. "We have lighting spells to relieve the darkness."

"We have lighting spells, too," Ilse said.

"And you should use them," Tir said. "But you'll find the Librarians have better ones."

"That's all the information I have now," Marlys said. "When I know anything more, I'll contact you again. If you have questions, you know where to reach me. But I think that you will have enough work to do reassuring everyone that this is not the end of the world, and brighter days will come again."

"Thank you," Durand said. "I want to offer my services if anyone needs help calming folk. I'm experienced at that."

Voni spoke up. "We may do that, Durand. I know that I speak for myself and other sorcerers in the regions that it's a pleasure to get acquainted with our fellow sorcerers who bring their unique talents and perspectives to our community."

Marlys heard sounds of assent.

"I'm confident that the sorcerers here that we feel the same towards you," Kayli said.

Again, Marlys heard sounds of agreement. “Thank you, Marlys,” Lindra added, “and may the Bright Beings bless your efforts.”

“May they look with favor on all of our efforts,” Marlys said. “I will leave you to your planning. Until we meet again, farewell.” Marlys closed the sorcerous connection.

Chapter 13

After Marlys ended the communication with the other sorcerers, Serena turned to Tir with a smile. “Light up the sky? That’s a spell I hadn’t read at the Library. I presume you’re willing to teach us?”

“Of course.” Tir reached for the spell book. “Slide the book, pen, and ink over to me and I’ll record it.”

“Did you ever try it?” Rochelle asked.

Tir shook his head as he dipped the pen in ink. “No, but Blair has, and he said it has amazing results.”

Celestine leaned toward Marlys and Tir. “Any other male sorcerers we don’t know about?”

“We only know of Tir and Blair and Durand,” Marlys said. “No one mentioned any others.”

“The one I’ve known up until now in my long life was a rogue, self-taught sorcerer,” Thorne said. “Not trained.”

Tir turned to her. “Perhaps if you bothered to train him, he wouldn’t have turned rogue.”

“We might have,” Thorne insisted, “*if* we had known about his existence before he began committing crimes. We have tried to find and query any child who can do household spells.”

“Maybe because you assumed there weren’t any,” Rochelle said, “you weren’t looking for them.”

Thorne threw Rochelle an exasperated look.

“I’ll take charge of sending out the sorcerers and apprentices here to tell the farmers and villagers in the vicinity of the fortress what to expect,” Celestine said.

“Thank you,” Marlys said. “I’d appreciate that.”

Most of the apprentices and sorcerers were back before the midday meal, reporting that they had not noticed any panic. Quite the contrary, the people seemed to have confidence that the sorcerers could all take care of everything.

"This is one instance where it's good that we're being taken for granted," Tir said as they cleaned up the luncheon dishes.

"Yes," Marlys said, "we want to avoid panic."

"I just hope that we can live up to their expectations," Rochelle said.

"What?" Thorne mocked. "The powerful Librarians doubt their abilities?"

"I think it's not a matter of 'if' we can resolve the crisis, but 'how well,'" Marlys said.

Thorne scoffed derisively.

The others exchanged glances but otherwise ignored her.

Astrid looked out the window as she was taking the cleaning rags back into the kitchen. "A horse and cart just appeared out of a distance-shortening spell. It seems to be Elspeth and her two young apprentices."

Thorne immediately turned and hurried out. Marlys followed at a more leisurely pace. Nessa joined Marlys as Marlys left the room. When they reached the door, they saw Elspeth stop the cart. Janna and Kelsie scrambled out and ran toward Thorne, who met them with open arms. She hugged them tightly.

"Oh!" Thorne said when she released the apprentices. "It's so good to see you! Have you been behaving yourselves?"

"Yes, High Sorcerer Thorne," they said.

Marlys lifted an eyebrow, but said nothing.

Elspeth tied the horse to a hitching post within reach of a water trough and hay before walking over to Thorne. They embraced.

"Good to see you, too!" Thorne said joyfully.

Marlys sensed Nessa moving next to her, and turned just in time to see Nessa cover her mouth and run off. After a glance toward Thorne, Marlys moved to follow.

Marlys found Nessa in one of the anterooms, leaning against a wall, weeping. She stepped to Nessa's side and pulled her into an embrace. Nessa did not resist, and continued to sob with her face buried in Marlys's shoulder.

When Nessa composed herself and pulled away gently, Marlys said, "That's the sort of reception you had hoped from your aunt. I can understand how hurt you must feel to see that affection directed to someone else."

Nessa sniffed and shook her head. “I don’t understand it.”

“I don’t, either,” Marlys said. “After all you did to help her.” When Nessa did not respond, continuing to shake her head, Marlys added, “How have you been getting along here?”

Nessa shrugged. “Well enough, I guess. Better than I expected, considering how fiercely I opposed you all trying to free my aunt.” She faced Marlys squarely. “You seem to have accepted me.”

Marlys smiled and patted Nessa’s arm. “The six of us are all Librarians now. That created a bond.”

“Celestine treats me and Zaria like all the other sorcerers here,” Nessa said.

“Of course,” Marlys said. “We sorcerers are a relatively small group. We need to watch out for each other and put our petty differences aside. None of us is perfect. Every one of us has an embarrassing mistake or two in our past.”

Nessa gestured toward the outside. “Except Aunt Thorne. She’s still carrying a grudge.”

Marlys sighed and nodded. “I’m giving it time. She may come around eventually. You did.”

“What if she doesn’t?” Nessa said bitterly.

“The world has already moved past her,” Marlys said. “From all the reports I’ve received throughout Goldenvalley, my former associates, Thorne’s former assembly members, have been working well with the ones I’ve trained. Thorne already knows that the other regions won’t allow her to return to her previous role. If she doesn’t adapt, she’ll be in a lonely place indeed.”

“...and a desperate one,” Nessa said.

“That’s the reason Serena, Tir, Rochelle and I have been keeping her under close observation,” Marlys said.

“If I see any sign of subterfuge from her,” Nessa said, “I’ll tell you, and Zaria would too, I know.”

“Thank you.” Marlys gestured to the door. “Let’s go get a cup of tea. I think we both need it.”

They walked quietly to the kitchen. No one else had remained there after the meal cleanup. Marlys stepped to a teapot kept warm by sorcery, and grasped the handle. She brought it to a small table with chairs in a corner, where Nessa had placed two empty cups. They sat in silence, sipping their tea.

Through the kitchen windows, they saw Tir instructing Rochelle and Zaria. Marlys presumed Serena was shadowing Thorne. The locator spell showed that she was in a meeting room, probably with Elspeth, Janna, and Kelsie.

When Marlys and Nessa had finished their tea, Marlys said, "Shall we go outside and see if we can learn how to light up the sky?" She went to the sink, and assisted by sorcery, washed, cleaned, and dried her cup before placing it on the counter.

"That would be quite a trick." Nessa cleaned her cup as well, and followed.

Outdoors, air was warm and the wind was gentle. Marlys looked up to see two pillars of light going up as far as she could see. The area around the fortress was lit as if it were noon on a sunny day.

"Once it's up, you just spread it out," Tir said. "But I don't recommend doing that now, because the villagers and farmers might worry about seeing a sudden light all around."

"Aren't they used to seeing sorcerous light here?" Nessa asked as she approached Tir.

Tir gestured toward the pillars of light. "They're used to seeing beacons in the direction of the fortress, yes, or light from the training centers. I don't think they're ready for a brilliant sky without the sun."

"At least," Marlys said, "we need to give the other sorcerers time to pass the word in their respective regions before making any widespread demonstrations."

Rochelle and Zaria canceled their spells. The light pillars vanished. The day turned dreary again.

"Ready to try it?" Tir asked Marlys and Nessa.

"Of course," Marlys said.

"That's what we came out for," Nessa said.

Rochelle and Zaria waved farewells and walked back to the fortress.

Tir gave Marlys and Nessa the instructions. Each cast the spell and two pillars of light appeared.

Tir smiled. "See? You're doing it."

"It's hard to keep the light from spreading," Nessa said.

"I think that's probably the point of the spell," Tir said.

Marlys and Nessa extinguished the lights.

"Very good," Tir said.

Marlys noticed movement out of the corner of her eye. She turned to look down the hill. Elspeth, Janna, and Kelsie walked toward the horse and cart, followed by Thorne.

Nessa, standing beside Marlys, let out a huff and strode back to the fortress's side door.

Meanwhile, Thorne hugged Elspeth, Janna, and Kelsie in turn. Elspeth untied the horse as the apprentices climbed into the cart. Then she took the reins, waved a farewell, and turned the horse toward the road. They disappeared into the distance-shortening spell. Thorne turned and walked back to the front door of the fortress with a smile on her face.

Tir looked from Thorne to Marlys. "That visit seemed to go well."

"Not for Nessa, though," Marlys said. "Seeing Thorne greet Elspeth and the others so warmly reminded her of what she hoped for and didn't get."

"It can't be easy for her," Tir said.

"She's adapting," Marlys said, "but it will take time." Checking the side door, she saw Serena, going out, passing Nessa, going back in.

When Serena reached them, she said, "Rochelle took over shadowing Thorne."

"Find out anything?" Tir asked.

"From what I heard where I sat in the next room," Serena said, "very little that we didn't know already. Janna and Kelsie talked about their training, Elspeth talked about informing the surrounding populace about the upcoming winter. Thorne was of the opinion that we Librarians would certainly fail to disperse the ash, and if we had any sense, we would realize that the only thing we could do is help people through the winter, and hope the ash would settle by spring or summer. Elspeth wondered what would happen if the ash didn't settle, and Thorne replied that there had been food shortages before. Rationing food would get us through until the sky returned to normal."

"If by this time next year, the ash doesn't settle, or we fail to disperse it, we may have to do that," Marlys said. "But there was a good harvest this autumn in the regions. The stored grains and plants should last us an entire year, or most of it. We have set aside even more food in storage in case of famine for a long time. We may not need to draw on our reserves."

"Thorne is of the opinion we ought to start now and we're fools if we don't," Serena said.

"We aren't at that point yet," Marlys said.

Serena nodded and crossed her arms in front of her. "I agree. Thorne isn't aware of all the choices available to us. Remember the waycakes?"

Tir's eyebrows went up. "For millions of people for months? How could we make that many?"

"As Marlys said," Serena answered, "we may only need to stretch our reserves by a small amount."

"But what of the ingredients?" Tir said. "We need a herb which only grows in the vicinity of Wishborne."

"Brianna gave us seeds," Serena said, "in case we could find a way to grow them. I believe that spells I read at the Library that can encourage plant growth would allow us to nurture and harvest the herb here."

Tir smiled. "That sounds promising."

"I'll talk to Celestine about putting together a work crew among the apprentices and sorcerers to build a greenhouse," Serena said.

"According to the spell book at the Library," Tir said, "the lighting spell is a good substitute for sunlight to grow plants, as well as for providing illumination."

Marlys smiled. "Excellent. This crisis is going to take all of us, each of us using our own special skills."

"Let's just hope that Thorne doesn't get in the way," Serena said.

After dinner that evening, Tir brought out a tray. Marlys recognized waycakes, cut into small pieces. He walked next to the tables where everyone still sat, lowering the tray so that it was within reach.

"These are waycakes," Tir said as he strolled along. "Take one. They're delicious."

Serena stood and addressed the assembly. "We found the recipe for this at Wishborne, along the Spell Passage. This is made up of the usual ingredients for breads and cakes, with the addition of a herb only grown there. It is possible to fortify the ingredients with sorcery. The preparation is complicated, but Marlys and I were able to make some."

As the sorcerers and apprentices sampled the waycakes, they smiled and nodded at each other.

"They're good!" Astrid said, and others made sounds of agreement.

Marlys saw Thorne take and eat a piece. She, too, seemed to enjoy it, smiling briefly, and then, as if realizing that she should not appear too enthusiastic, her face returned to its usual somber expression.

"All of us who traveled to the Library came away with extra waycakes," Serena said. "They don't spoil, and just one of these waycakes is enough for a meal."

Thorne turned to her. "Do you have the ability to make thousands of these at a time? Thousands upon thousands is what we would need to feed the continent for any significant length of time."

"We don't have that ability, true," Marlys said. "But we may be able to make enough to help a small area for a brief time while we're gathering other resources."

Thorne smirked and shook her head.

Serena turned to her. "It is not wise to overlook the value of small efforts. They can sometimes make a large difference."

Thorne sipped her tea and made no answer.

Chapter 14

While waiting for the Librarians to give them instructions about how to deal with the ash, the sorcerers in Goldenvalley, as the sorcerers everywhere else, worked at their usual tasks. Marlys and Celestine tutored apprentices. They sent sorcerers and apprentices out to heal injuries or clear and repair wreckages, among other sorcerous duties. Occasionally, Marlys or Celestine went out themselves.

Thorne remained at the fortress, still under surveillance. If she was aware of being shadowed, she gave no sign. Serena, Tir, and Rochelle reported that she spent most of her time reading spell books and searching for hidden spells. Sometimes she would stand outside in the open, casting spells as if she were throwing out a fishing line. Serena believed that Thorne's purpose was to try to invent new spells, though neither she nor anyone else observed any significant results.

Serena continued to tutor Lyra, who would go from one place to another with Serena or other sorcerers and teach those who could do household spells how to better produce light or flames. That seemed to help relieve the pervasive gloom, though only at a local level.

Marlys, Serena, and a couple of other sorcerers knew enough about construction to put together a small greenhouse, where Serena started growing the Windborne herb.

Marlys continued to send and receive messages from the Library of Sorcery and from elsewhere around the continent. After about a month of darkness, the weather gradually but definitely turning cold, Marlys called a meeting of those at the fortress.

"I think it's time for me, and the other Librarians here, to light up the sky," she said. "Everyone's reporting that the citizens in their area are getting weary of the gloom."

Tir nodded. "How are we going to do this?"

Nessa had made a quick trip to the Library of Sorcery and returned with a detailed map of the continent. It had been laid out on a table in the dining hall.

"We need to spread out as much as we can," Marlys said. "I'll stay here. Rochelle, do you want to take the coastlands?"

Rochelle nodded.

Marlys gestured at Tir. "Do you want to take the mining regions? You can visit Durand while you're in the area."

Before Tir could respond, Nessa spoke up. "Zaria and I are banished from the regions, remember? Since we can't go there, wouldn't it make more sense for one of us to go to the mining regions, and the other to the Spell Passage?"

"I was hoping to go to the Spell Passage," Serena said.

"I talk to Durand regularly through the sorcerous channels," Tir said. "Nessa's right, it makes more sense for her or Zaria to go to the mining regions."

"All right." Marlys turned to Zaria. "Zaria, would you be willing to go to the mining regions?"

"Of course," Zaria said.

"Nessa, would you be willing to take the long journey to the islands?"

"Yes, I can do that," Nessa said.

Marlys consulted the map and pointed out a location. "Tir, you go here. That should close the gap between here, the western coastlands, the southern mining areas, and the Spell Passage. Serena can take that area."

"What about the far northeast?" Zaria asked.

"The Librarians have tenuous contacts there. Genevieve will send one of their sorcerers, and they will illuminate the Library district."

Nessa faced Tir. "How does this work again?"

"Send up the light," Tir said, "and give it all the power you can. It should spread out on its own."

"How long does it last?" Serena asked.

"According to Blair, and what I've read, half a day before the light gradually fades," Tir said. "You can cast the spell and then come back if you wish."

"...or stay and watch for a while, if you want to," Marlys said.

"Shall we go now?" Serena said.

"No reason not to," Marlys said.

After the other Librarians left, Marlys stepped outside to cast the spell. She wore a jacket against the chill. Everyone else, including Thorne, followed her and stood in a group in front of her to watch. The wind, though not strong, was brisk. Apprentices tucked their hair behind their ears to keep it from blowing into their mouths. Sorcerers generally chose to keep their hair short, but the gusts still played with their curls and bangs. Everyone's skirts or pant legs flapped in the breeze. The sorcerers huddled around the apprentices, keeping them all warm through sorcery. Even so, most pulled their jackets around them to keep the wind out.

Marlys looked up, seeing nothing but gray. She cast the spell, lifting her arms as if throwing the light towards the sky. A wide pillar of light appeared, reached the clouds, and started to spread in all directions. Eventually the pillars lifted off the ground and shot into the sky, blending with the canopy.

Looking down again, she saw the others gazing upward.

"It's not a warm light, is it?" Celestine said.

"No." Marlys slowly turned around. "But it has seemed to travel to the horizon and beyond."

"The sky is bright, but still gray," Astrid said. "I miss blue."

"It's nice just for the outside to be brighter," Esme said. "Everything seemed so dim."

"I wonder what those living in remote areas think of this new overhead glow," Oriana said.

"Probably the same when they see sorcerous lights in the distance," Thorne said. "When I was a little girl, my father would look at lights on the horizon and say, 'The sorcerers are at it again. Just ignore it.' But I was fascinated enough to want to become one."

"My Dad would tell us that it was the Bright Beings having a celebration," Astrid said.

"My grandma would say that about the dancing lights in the northern sky," Celestine said. "With sorcerous lights, she'd tell me that it was sorcerers at work to protect us and help us."

Marlys scanned the horizon for a few moments more, then said, "Tir said this should last for a while, then slowly fade. In the meantime, I'm getting out of the wind."

Some followed her back inside. Others stayed out longer to watch the glow.

Tir returned to the fortress first, stepping through the end of the transportation spell inside the audience hall, where the others waited.

He grinned. "Success!"

Zaria returned next. "The light is up."

Rochelle came in soon afterwards. "Everything went as planned. The sorcerers there extend their thanks."

Nessa's image appeared. "The light is working over the islands. With your permission, Marlys, I'd like to stay a day or two longer. They're still rebuilding and cleaning up here. I realized that there's much I can do to hurry things along."

"Do you need help?" Marlys asked.

"No," Nessa said. "Everyone's sheltered, at least temporarily, and everyone's being fed. They say the fish are still taking the bait and their bees are still making honey. The sorcerers here have been working hard and I can give them some relief and rest."

Marlys nodded. "Stay as long as you need to. Call if we can assist in any way."

"I will." Nessa's image faded.

Privately, Marlys wondered whether Nessa just needed to stay out of Thorne's vicinity for a time.

Serena came through the transportation spell from Wishborne with Brianna. Brianna carried a travel bag.

Marlys stepped forward with a smile. "Brianna! Good to see you!" She took Brianna's hand briefly in welcome.

"We enlisted Durand to mind Wishborne for a time," Serena said. "I asked Brianna to come here to tell us if the herbs are maturing well, and to see if we can make waycakes here."

"I have been making waycakes at Wishborne from the time I heard from you about the coming long winter," Brianna said. "But if it's possible for other sites to make them, we would be much better prepared."

“Would you be willing to teach a class?” Marlys said. “I can contact the sorcerers in the other regions again and ask, if it’s possible for them to do so, for each of them to send a sorcerer here for instruction.”

“I’m willing,” Brianna said, “but I wish to determine whether we can make waycakes here first.”

“Of course,” Marlys said.

“I’ll get Brianna settled in a room,” Serena said.

“Please do,” Marlys said.

At the midday meal, Serena sat to Brianna’s left. Thorne squeezed in next to Brianna on the right. Marlys sat across the table from Brianna. Serena threw Marlys an exasperated look. Brianna’s attention, at least at that moment, seemed to be on her meal.

“I traveled through the Spell Passage in my younger days,” Thorne said, turning to Brianna. “But a sorcerer named Lariss was at Wishborne then.”

Brianna nodded and glanced toward Thorne. “Yes, she was my predecessor there. She trained me as a station host. We both lived at Wishborne for a year.”

“It must have been awkward,” Thorne said, “with those glowing stones inhibiting sorcery if more than one sorcerer is present.”

“Not really,” Brianna said as she dipped her fork into the mashed potatoes on her plate, “if we needed to use sorcery, one or the other of us would simply step away for a brief time.” She looked over at Marlys. “These potatoes are delicious. Lightly buttered and seasoned, good consistency.”

Marlys gestured. “Those are Celestine’s specialty. We look forward to them when she’s on kitchen duty.”

Brianna turned to Celestine. “My compliments.”

Celestine smiled. “Thank you.”

“Lariss made waycakes for me and my companion, Sorcerer Elspeth,” Thorne continued, as if her conversation had not been interrupted. “She showed us how she made them, but we weren’t able to make them ourselves.”

“That’s not a failing,” Brianna said. “I had to watch Lariss make them more than once before I had success. Even experienced sorcerers have not been able to duplicate the process."

"I am very experienced," Thorne said with a glance toward Marlys, "having served as High Sorcerer here for many years."

Serena looked around Brianna to Thorne. "Marlys and I were able to make waycakes successfully after Brianna taught us."

Thorne turned to Serena. "I'm sure that Brianna will be able to teach more of us here, in our own kitchen."

"That's what I came here for," Brianna said.

"I look forward to it." Thorne settled back in her chair with a self-satisfied grin.

After the meal, Serena escorted Brianna to the greenhouse. Marlys and Tir walked with them. Thorne tagged along behind them.

Once inside, Tir kindled a sorcerous light. Serena showed Brianna the two long planting troughs filled with soil. Marlys saw sprouts growing in both. The plants in one trough had grown taller than the plants in the other trough.

"On this side," Serena said, "I planted seeds and am allowing them to grow naturally. On the other side, I planted seeds and have used sorcery to speed growth. The Librarians tell me there shouldn't be difference in them, but I thought it would be best to plant two rows in the event sorcery affected their properties."

Brianna turned to Serena. "You were able to accelerate plant growth with a spell? Can you use it on an entire field?"

Serena shook her head. "I can only cast a spell on one plant at a time."

Brianna walked over to one of the taller plants, bent down, and fingered the leaves. "Do you cast the spell once per plant or does the spell have to be renewed?"

"Once," Serena said. "The plant grows faster than usual until it reaches maturity."

Brianna looked from the plant to Serena and back again. "This one seems to have attained its full growth."

"We were wondering about seeds," Marlys said. "We wanted to be sure we had seeds to continue planting."

Brianna nodded. "The leaves are where we get the herb from. The seeds are right here, in these small pods." She touched the plant again.

"Are the seeds mature and ready for replanting?" Marlys asked.

After carefully opening a pod, Brianna said, "The seeds are mature, too. I'd gather them and set them aside for planting later."

"Can you show us how to harvest the herbs and seeds?" Serena asked.

Tir pointed to a stand. "Gardening tools and containers are over there."

"Let's get started," Brianna said.

Chapter 15

Marlys, Serena, Tir, and Thorne all gathered around Brianna as she put on gardening gloves and grasped the gardening shears. She showed them how to harvest the herbs and gather the seeds. Marlys glanced at Thorne now and again. Thorne had remained silent throughout, but her face showed that she was listening intently. Marlys wondered whether Thorne was truly interested in the process, or taking note of the surroundings in order to undermine their efforts later.

When Brianna felt she had sufficient herbs to start cooking, they returned to the fortress. Once they reached the dining hall next to the kitchen, Marlys saw that all the sorcerers and apprentices had gathered, waiting for them.

"Are you going to make the waycakes now?" Esme asked. "Can we watch?"

"We can't all comfortably fit in the kitchen at once," Marlys said.

"Rochelle and I have already observed the process," Tir said. "We can stay here."

Rochelle nodded.

Brianna gestured toward Marlys and Serena. "Marlys and Serena already have successfully made waycakes. I know that they would be happy to show any of you at any time. Right now, I just want to see if we can successfully make them here."

"If I understand correctly," Thorne said, "the plan is for a number of sorcerers to come here to learn the technique, if successful here. There will be many opportunities to learn."

Marlys took a moment to wonder what Thorne was up to before saying, "We'll only have sorcerers in the kitchen for now, except for Lyra, who can watch and share information with the apprentices."

"Can apprentices make it?" Oriana asked.

"If they have access to ingredients already fortified by sorcery," Brianna said. "Even if we aren't successful here, I want other sorcerers to know how to do that. They could then bring those ingredients to me at Wishborne so that I have larger quantities to work with."

"Let's start, then," Marlys said. "Apprentices, outside. All sorcerers, remain here until all the ingredients are fortified."

"I have the recipe memorized," Brianna said. "I can call out the ingredients."

Marlys reached for the shelf with the cookbooks. "I have a written copy of the recipe here." She took out a paper and put it on the central counter in the kitchen. "We can use that for reference, but go ahead and call out the ingredients. We'll gather them."

Everyone had worked in the kitchen before, if not as a cook, then as an assistant. When Brianna called out an ingredient, Marlys gestured to a sorcerer, who found the ingredient in the cabinets and brought it to the counter. She directed a few sorcerers to find a second ingredient.

When she reached the end of the list, Brianna looked around at the jars and containers of ingredients on the counter, lids off. "The reason Marlys asked you to take only one or two ingredients is that we have to fortify only one ingredient at a time. This is not a spell to do all at once, and the recipe will fail if that happens."

"What does 'fail' mean?" Thorne asked. "Is the result poisonous?"

"Not at all," Brianna said. "Failed waycakes are still cakes, and if prepared competently, can be delicious. But they won't have waycake properties." She looked around again. "Watch as I cast the spell to fortify the flour in front of me. You'll see how I limit the magic to the one ingredient."

"Can you over- or under-fortify?" Thorne asked.

"No," Brianna said. "The spell either works or it doesn't. If it works, the ingredient will be warm for a few moments. If it doesn't, the ingredient will be cool."

Thorne nodded.

Marlys caught Serena's eye and lifted an eyebrow. Thorne's were good questions. Whatever her attitude, Thorne was an experienced sorcerer and it showed.

"Clean your hands before casting the spell," Brianna said. "We'll start handling the ingredients soon." After everyone in the room used the simple cleaning spell, Brianna cast the spell to fortify the flour in front of her. The others watched, then imitated the spell on the ingredients in front of them. Those with more than one ingredient cast it twice.

“Everyone succeed?” Brianna asked.

The other sorcerers answered with nods or sounds of assent.

“We’ll leave the kitchen,” Tir said. He and Rochelle walked to the door. The apprentices, clustered at the doorway, gave way and came together again. Marlys saw that a couple of apprentices had apparently retrieved stools to stand on, so they could see over the heads of those standing in front of them.

After exchanging a nod with Marlys, Serena said, “Marlys and I will retire to the kitchen table to give the rest of you room to watch.”

“We can make four small batches with what we have,” Brianna said. “I’ll take one, and three of you can see if you can make a batch yourself.”

At first, the sorcerers simply looked from one to the other.

“I just want to watch for now, if that’s all right,” Esme said. Other sorcerers nodded.

“If you’ll take an apprentice, I want to try,” Lyra said.

Brianna smiled. “Of course.”

“I’d like to see if I can do it,” Thorne said.

“That’s two,” Brianna said. “Anyone else?”

A couple of sorcerers pushed Celestine playfully.

“Come on, Celestine,” Astrid said. “You try it.”

“I was going to give the rest of you a chance,” Celestine said.

“No, we really want to see you try it,” Esme said.

Celestine smiled, spread her hands, and stepped forward.

From her chair at the corner of the kitchen, Marlys watched as Brianna explained the complex mixing, sifting, and shaping process of the batter. The sorcerers not doing preparation gave the cooks room to maneuver, but watched closely. At the doorway, Marlys saw that Tir and Rochelle also appeared to have retrieved stools so they could stand on them and watch over the heads of the clustered apprentices.

At last, the rounds of waycake batter were placed on baking sheets and then into the oven. Brianna explained that for the waycakes to come out properly, they would have to avoid speeding the baking process with sorcery. In the meantime, she instructed the others to gather the fortified ingredients and set them aside in marked containers for future attempts.

As they worked, the fragrant aroma of waycake filled the kitchen.

“Mmmm.” Lyra turned to Brianna. “Marlys and the others shared waycake samples with us earlier. It smells as good as it tastes.”

The baking process did not last overly long. Brianna took out the baking sheets and set them on the counter. “They need to rest for a few minutes. We can eat or store them once they are cooler.”

“They need no spells to preserve them?” Thorne asked.

Brianna nodded. “That’s the point. To have food that can serve as a meal that can be taken anywhere, anytime, with no preparation.”

“Whatever we don’t sample now,” Marlys said, “we’ll put in containers and store them in the fortress to use at need.”

“Can we come in now?” Oriana asked.

Marlys waved them in. They all crowded around the central counter.

Brianna took a knife and cut one of her own waycakes into pieces. She put one in her mouth, chewed, swallowed, and nodded. “Success!”

The others cheered and applauded.

Brianna distributed the other pieces and moved to Celestine’s batch. Again, she cut up a waycake, tasted it, and passed the other pieces to those nearby.

“Is it a waycake?” Marlys asked.

Brianna put a hand on Celestine’s shoulder. “Yes! Congratulations!”

Again, the statement was met with applause and cheers.

Brianna went to Lyra’s batch next. Lyra’s eyes were downcast, as if expecting a reprimand. When Brianna ate a piece of one of Lyra’s waycakes, and smiled, Lyra looked up hopefully.

“You did it!” Brianna said to Lyra.

Lyra’s face brightened at the applause of the others.

Last of all, Brianna cut up one of Thorne’s cakes. Thorne stood by, wearing a wide, confident smile as Brianna ate a piece. Thorne took one of the pieces herself and ate it.

Brianna swallowed and nodded. "It's good."

Thorne smirked.

"However," Brianna added, "it isn't a waycake."

Thorne's smile dimmed, but only slightly.

Brianna touched Thorne's arm. "It's still good, though. Having eaten many failed waycakes, mine as well as those of others, this tastes as if the ingredients were slightly out of balance. The cakes are fine, they just aren't waycakes."

"I wanted to add a touch of creativity," Thorne said.

"Nothing wrong with that," Brianna said, "as long as you realize that the results will be different."

Thorne took another knife and cut other cakes of hers into pieces. She put them on a plate and walked around, distributing them. Most of the others took a piece, including Marlys, who found the cake delicious. Others nodded or voiced their approvals as well.

Serena cleared her throat and reached for a ceramic container. "Unless you want some to take home with you," she said to Brianna, "I'll gather the waycakes and store them properly."

"Since they were made with your ingredients, it's only fair that you use them as you wish," Brianna said.

Having given away all the pieces on her plate, Thorne found a smaller container for the remaining cakes that she had baked. "I'll preserve these and set them aside for a later date."

No one commented as Thorne filled her container and left.

Serena, Marlys, and Brianna wrapped the remaining waycakes individually and placed them in Serena's container. As they did so, Celestine turned to the others in the kitchen. "Good work, all. Now we need to attend to our usual duties."

Everyone left except Brianna and the Librarians in the room.

Once the waycakes had been placed in the container, Serena closed and sealed the lid. In a low voice, she said, "I'm placing these in a lower level of the fortress under the protective spell I learned at the Library of Sorcery."

"Good idea," Tir said.

After Serena left, Marlys turned to Brianna. "We also now know that we can produce a waycake using a herb whose growth has been accelerated by sorcery."

Brianna nodded. “That’s hopeful. And that will allow us to produce a great many more waycakes than we otherwise would.”

“That may well make a difference between getting through the winter comfortably or having to suffer great hardship,” Tir said.

“Speaking of the spells you learned at the Library of Sorcery,” Brianna said, “can any sorcerer do them?”

“Some any sorcerer can do,” Marlys said. “Others take the strength of a Librarian. The transportation spell that Serena used to bring you here is one of those.”

Brianna nodded.

“But they have no recipe or technique for waycakes,” Marlys said. “I asked. They were quite in awe of them.”

Brianna smiled.

“The sorcery we’ve practiced here has served us well for centuries,” Tir said. “We have no need to be ashamed, or think that what we did was lesser.”

“I don’t, I assure you,” Brianna said, “but I can’t help but wonder if the sorcerous strength we have among us will be sufficient to carry us through the current crisis.”

“It will,” Marlys said confidently. “It must. It may take all of us doing what we can, but I see no reason for despair.”

“Despair, no,” Brianna said. “Every sorcerer I’ve talked to is ready to meet this crisis with all of our strength, and more. I wondered, though, whether it’s possible to share the Library’s knowledge more widely.”

Rochelle crossed her arms in front of her. “It’s not a matter of being willing. You’re more than welcome to read our spell books and see what Serena’s recorded so far. The difficulty is that there are so many spells in the Library, it would take more than a lifetime to learn them. We only learned a fraction of them. Serena learned more, but even she did not absorb the knowledge of the entire Library.”

“We won’t hesitate to share any spell that might be useful,” Marlys said.

“The problem there,” Brianna said, “is that it may not be obvious as to what is useful and what is not. There have been many times since my sorcery has awakened when what I thought was a minor or trivial spell turned out to be something I urgently needed.”

“I agree,” Marlys said. “But the obstacle of volume remains.”

“I have an idea,” Zaria said, speaking for the first time. “We can reserve a time each evening to open the sorcerous channels to all the sorcerous locations and read a spell that any sorcerer could do. Since it takes a Librarian to reach everyone at once, I’d be willing to do that.”

Brianna turned to her, “I know I and other sorcerers would be grateful if you would.”

“Excellent idea,” Marlys said. “Thank you for volunteering.”

Brianne took a deep breath, and smiled. “I’m grateful for your hospitality, but I’d better get back to Wishborne...after taking a little more time to read your spell books, of course.”

“Of course,” Marlys said. “And I understand. Thank you for your help here.”

“I’m glad to give it,” Brianna said. “As you pointed out, it’s going to take all of us to meet this crisis.”

Chapter 16

Two days later, after Brianna had returned to Wishborne, and Nessa came back from the Islands, Elspeth arrived with other sorcerers around the region and from nearby regions to learn how to make waycakes.

After the instruction ended, the visiting sorcerers returned home, except for Elspeth. She stayed behind and talked to Thorne in the high sorcerer's suite. Marlys sat in her study in the next room, copying the waycake recipe. Neither made a move to close the door, and Marlys did not, either.

"Well, did you succeed?" Thorne asked.

"Surprisingly, yes," Elspeth said. "I never considered myself more than an adequate cook. Some of the others failed, however."

"What a waste of time," Thorne said.

"As I understand it, one small waycake is as good as a meal, and doesn't require sorcery to preserve it. I think that's an accomplishment."

"I don't care what they say," Thorne said. "I thought it was a fraud back when you and I stopped at Wishborne on our journey through the Spell Passage, and I still think so. A cake that has such properties only if you make it a certain way? Nonsense. When I was growing up, my mother and grandfather would prepare breads and cakes only by measuring with cupped hands. Undoubtedly, the measurements were not exactly the same each time, and still, the food came out good regardless."

"You never know with magic," Elspeth said. "Even without magic, Filix once told me, when I sent back bread that tasted flat, that the cook had missed a tiny amount of some ingredient. I forget which."

"I still think it's nonsense," Thorne said.

"It could be," Elspeth said. "But if the waycakes do what they claim they do, they may save us from famine if the winter becomes as harsh as predicted."

"Exactly my point," Thorne said, "we can't base our survival on a couple of cakes. It would be better if we started rationing now. But no one listens to me."

"If we reach that point, I'm sure they will," Elspeth said.

"By the time they do, it'll be too late, and they will rue the day they decided to ignore me."

"I don't think they're ignoring you," Elspeth said. "From what I hear, you're still a part of the daily activities here."

"Yes, but they watch me closely, and don't think I haven't noticed that."

"Trust takes time," Elspeth said.

"You'd think I'd earned it by now, as long as I have been High Sorcerer here."

"Most here have few memories of you," Elspeth said.

"Memories warped by certain parties, no doubt," Thorne said.

"They're giving you a chance," Elspeth said. "They could have forbidden you to try the waycake recipe, and they didn't."

"Hm," Thorne said. "I'll give them that. But still...."

"Things will work out for the best," Elspeth said. "They usually do."

Thorne said nothing in response.

"Come, see me to the door," Elspeth said. "I need to get back."

Marlys heard footsteps as they left the room.

The next day, Genevieve's image appeared in the dining hall as they were cleaning up after breakfast.

After exchanging greetings with Marlys, Genevieve said, "Our skywatchers believe they have found a spell that can help disperse the ash."

Many in the room cheered.

"Before you get your hopes up, the skywatchers believe dispersing this much ash will take time, perhaps until spring. But we can make a start."

The room quieted.

"Does it take the strength of a Librarian, or can any sorcerer cast this spell?" Marlys asked.

"That's the other restriction," Genevieve said. "Only Librarians can cast the spell. Blair wishes to come to instruct you and answer your questions."

"Of course." Marlys heard excited gasps, especially from the apprentices.

"What time would be convenient for you?"

Marlys scanned the faces of the other Librarians in the room. "Anytime. We're ready now."

"Good. He'll come soon. Until then, may the blessings of the Bright Beings remain with you."

"With you also," Marlys said as Genevieve's image faded.

"A Librarian from the Library of Sorcery coming here!" Oriana said with a grin.

"Marlys, can we stay and watch?" Lyra asked.

"Yes, of course you can stay," Marlys said.

Thorne turned to the apprentices. "A Librarian is just a sorcerer, nothing more. You'd think that one of the Bright Beings was coming from the way you're carrying on."

Marlys saw no diminishment of the apprentices' excitement. They were bouncing up and down energetically and clapping their hands. The sorcerers who had never been to the Library had eager smiles on their faces.

Moments later, Blair stepped out of the transportation spell. Tir walked to him immediately and embraced him. When they parted, Marlys made introductions.

Blair motioned to the tables. "May I sit and explain?"

"Please do," Marlys said.

All the Librarians sat next to and across from Blair. Other sorcerers and apprentices remained standing, clustering around the Librarians. Thorne took a seat within sight but not close by.

"We found a spell that will disperse the ash," Blair said. "This was tricky, because simply moving it around won't work. It's everywhere. Moving one section of ash in the sky to another place in the sky simply has ash elsewhere coming in to fill the gap."

"I take it you tried," Thorne called from her seat.

Blair turned to her briefly. "Yes." He turned back to Marlys and company. "We don't want to create an ash fall, at least not all at once, or everything will be covered by it, more than we can manage at one time."

"The islands are already coping with ash fall," Rochelle said.

"And there's still enough ash above them to block sunlight," Nessa added.

"Destroying it can be done," Blair said, "but only in small amounts, because it takes so much energy."

"You could increase the number of Librarians," Thorne said.

"If every sorcerer on this world became a Librarian, it would not be enough." Blair shifted his weight in the chair. "What we can do, at least for now, is pulverize the ash, in whatever small amounts we can, and bring that down to a level where it meets the prevailing wind currents above. Some may fall locally with the snow, but most of it should be carried out by the wind to the sea and rain down there."

"Would the snow and rain be fit to drink?" Marlys asked.

"The transformed ash would be no more harmful than if soil got into the water," Blair said. "Nearly all the people in the Library district, and here, too, I understand, get drinking water from wells or springs, which is filtered in the ground."

"I was thinking about animals. Animals and people sometimes drink from steams," Marlys said.

"When we tested it in the Library district," Blair said, "there was a tiny amount of debris in the water, but nothing that affected anyone badly. When I tried it, it tasted like mineral water. Some said they couldn't taste a difference at all."

"At least you had the presence of mind to try it on yourself first, rather than having others discover any possible harmful effects," Thorne said.

Blair turned to her. "We always do that. Don't you?"

Thorne did not answer.

"Yes," Marlys said, "it's usual for us to try spells on ourselves first here, too."

Blair put his hands on the table. "If you're ready, we can go outside and I'll demonstrate the spell."

They all stood. Some of the apprentices let out tiny squeals of delight. Blair smiled at them as he followed Marlys to the door.

When they had gathered outside, apprentices outfitted in jackets and coats, Blair stepped away from the group, looked up, and then back at the onlookers. "Here's what you do." Lifting his arms and facing upwards, he cast the spell.

Everyone scanned the sky directly above them.

"I don't see anything," Oriana said.

"We sorcerers can, with the far-seeing spell," Tir said. "I can see a swirling action and what appears to be silvery rain coming down, and then surging to the east, as if following a river of air."

"That's a fair description of what's happening," Blair said.

"Again," Thorne said, "why not create more Librarians and get more done?"

"Whether ash or pulverized ash," Blair said, "I assure you, you don't want it coming down all at once."

"Particles that small can get into the lungs," Rochelle said, "you wouldn't want to breathe that."

"Whether it's ash or sand or something smaller," Nessa said, "it would still pile up and get into everything, not only outside, but into houses and barns and storage bins." She faced Thorne. "If you want that, Aunt Thorne, you can be the one to clean it up."

Thorne only shook her head.

Blair seemed to pretend not to notice the exchange. He turned to Marlys. "Now your group can try it."

"Do we take turns, or do we all cast the spell at once?" Serena asked.

"Best you do it individually," Blair said, "so I can watch and advise."

Marlys stepped forward first. Following Blair's instructions, she cast the spell. After checking the sky, Blair nodded approval.

Stepping back to let the other Librarians cast the spell, Marlys noticed that one of the apprentices had produced a spyglass. They passed it from one to the other to observe the result. The sorcerers who were not Librarians murmured among themselves, fingers pointing at the clouds.

Tir was the last in line. Once he had cast his spell, Blair watched for results and clapped a hand on his shoulder. "Good." He faced the others. "You all did well. Genevieve is working on a plan to schedule all the Librarians so that we can spread out and work the spell at intervals."

"We'll await her word," Marlys said.

Blair scanned the faces of the observers. "As delighted as I am to make your acquaintance, I need to get back. I'm continuing my research to see if I can find an even better spell."

"May the Bright Beings guide you," Marlys said. "Please let us know if we can be of assistance."

"Thank you." Blair cast the transportation spell and stepped through the portal.

Thorne turned to the apprentices, all of whom were smiling. "See? He was just an ordinary sorcerer."

Serena walked between Thorne and the apprentices on her way back to the fortress. "It is unwise to judge the strength or ability of a sorcerer based on appearances."

The apprentices giggled and ran ahead of Serena as a group to get back inside the fortress, and warmth.

Thorne let out a long breath and followed.

Marlys turned to the sorcerers. "We've made a start."

The first flakes of snow fell outside the window as everyone ate their supper in the dining hall. The apprentices gathered at the windows and discussed whether enough would fall by the next day for sledding down the hill the fortress was built on.

Tir, remaining seated with the other sorcerers, said, "Our first snow is early."

"I've seen snow this early before," Thorne said. "More than once."

"I'd wonder if this was a sign of a harsh winter," Celestine said, "but my grandparents used to say that the date of the first snow has little to do whether the winter will be mild or severe."

"We'll just have to wait and see," Marlys said, "and hope the winter is not severe beyond our ability to deal with it."

Chapter 17

The next morning, when Marlys sat down to breakfast, she looked around and saw no apprentices at the table, only sorcerers.

"They were all up early," Celestine said with a smile, "ate a quick breakfast, bundled up with coats, boots, hats, and mittens, and rushed outside with sleds and toboggans."

"How much snow did we get?" Marlys asked.

"Over my ankles," Celestine said.

Marlys took a deep breath and let it out. "We'll have to clear the roads in the vicinity, then."

"How do you do that?" Zaria asked. "I haven't done that before. I don't remember being instructed."

"It's essentially like mucking out the barn," Marlys said, "where we push the manure out and into a pile to use in our garden and orchard later."

Thorne cast her eyes to the ceiling and clicked her tongue. She faced Marlys. "If you had but refrained from your time-binding spell for a season more, Elspeth or I would have shown you the right way to clear the roads."

Marlys turned to Thorne and looked her in the eye. "I'm willing to learn now."

Thorne paused a moment before answering. "It's a two-step process. First, you lighten the snow. You know how some snow is fluffy and other snow is heavy and sticks together well, for making snowballs, for instance."

Marlys nodded.

"The first spell," Thorne continued, "is to take enough moisture out of the snow to make it extra fluffy. The second spell lifts the snow and sets it aside. Easier than doing it your way, and you don't come home exhausted after the roads are clear."

"Excellent," Marlys said. "Can you show us after breakfast?"

"So you admit I might know a thing or two about sorcery after all?" Thorne challenged.

"You have years of experience and practice," Marlys said. "Of course I realize you know details about sorcery that the rest of us don't."

Thorne inclined her head in answer and turned her attention to the eggs on her plate. Marlys, who had excellent hearing, caught her mumbling to herself, "Might have admitted it in the first place."

After the sorcerers were finished eating, they all pitched in to clean up, silently consenting to allow the apprentices on kitchen duty that day to have the morning off.

Even with sorcery to warm them, the sorcerers still donned jackets and hats to go outside. They grabbed mittens and boots as well.

Once outfitted, they all gathered outside the fortress entrance. The apprentices approached them, hauling their sleds and toboggans behind them, steam issuing from their mouths and noses.

"Do you want to go sledding, too?" Oriana asked the assembled sorcerers.

"I thought we might teach a lesson," Marlys said.

The apprentices groaned softly.

Marlys smiled. "Don't worry, it won't interfere with your fun. We'll slide downhill, and then show you how sorcerers clear snow."

The apprentices cheered.

There were sufficient toboggans for the sorcerers to crowd onto them, though apprentices took the first and last positions.

Then they were off. Marlys felt the thrill of speed and of the wind in her face as they sped down the hill. Too soon, it seemed, they reached the bottom. The toboggans slowed on the level surface until softly blocked by a snowbank.

Marlys stood and brushed snow off her clothes. Nearby, she saw Thorne, looking almost as pleased as the apprentices, step off a toboggan.

"Now I will show you the proper way to clear a road with sorcery," Thorne said, facing the others.

Surprised that Thorne, and not Marlys or Celestine or Serena, was giving a lesson, the apprentices turned to Marlys, who nodded. At Marlys's affirmation, all turned their attention to Thorne.

Thorne explained and demonstrated the spells. When she cast the first spell, steam rose from the blanket of snow. At the second spell, the snow rose up and to the side spectacularly, like a wave crashing on rocks. Within moments, the path from the main road to the fortress entrance had been cleared.

The onlookers gasped in appreciation.

Thorne faced the group with a satisfied grin.

Marlys raised her arms. "Now, the rest of us sorcerers can take a small strip of road and try it."

One by one, each sorcerer cast the spell on a part of the road. Soon, the main road was clear on either direction as far as the eye could see.

"Very good," Marlys said. "Now the sorcerers among us can shorten distances and clear our usual assigned sections of road."

"Oh, let's take at least one more run down the hill first," Nessa said.

"It'll take a while to trudge up the hill again," Lyra said.

Nessa smiled. "I think we can get us there faster."

"There's not enough room for the distance-shortening spell," Esme said.

"Who said I was going to cast a distance-shortening spell?" Nessa said playfully. She described a glowing circle and gestured toward it. "Step inside."

The apprentices all turned from one to the other with skeptical expressions.

Tir chuckled and pointed to Serena, Zaria, and Rochelle. "We'll go first. We've done this before."

The four sorcerers lined up and walked in. Almost immediately, a glowing circle formed near the fortress entrance. All stepped out of the circle and waved back.

Marlys glanced at Thorne, who wore an astonished expression. Apparently she felt such spells were beyond her niece's ability.

"This is a spell Nessa invented herself," Marlys explained.

"Are you going to teach it to us?" Astrid asked carefully.

"I'd be happy to," Nessa said, "but please step through first so I can close the circle."

The rest of them scrambled in, sorcerers, apprentices, toboggans and all. Nessa stepped through last and closed the end point.

“You have got to teach us this,” Celestine said.

“I need to rest a few moments after casting this one,” Nessa said. “Shall we save the lesson for this afternoon?”

“Besides, after we reach the bottom of the hill again, the sorcerers will be clearing roads,” Marlys said. “Thorne, Nessa, and I will take the immediate roads. Everyone else, clear where you were assigned last winter.”

After the midday meal, they gathered outside again. Marlys and Serena stood back because they had already learned the end point spell. The apprentices gathered closer, but at a respectful distance to leave room for the sorcerers to gather around Nessa.

As Nessa gave her instruction, Serena leaned toward Marlys and said in a low voice, “Thorne seems to be taking an intense interest in this particular spell. Thinking of escape, maybe?”

Marlys turned to Serena. “She’s not a prisoner, you know. Even if she leaves, she can’t hide from the locator spell. We can go after her and retrieve her at any time, and she knows that.”

“Still, she could create a lot of mischief. She could leave the fortress while we’re all asleep. That would give her some time before we detected her absence and followed.”

“I don’t know anywhere Thorne could go and hide. Even Thorne’s former assembly members wouldn’t be inclined to conspire with her to overthrow me, I would think. The reports I’m getting from them show that they’re essentially of the same mind as Elspeth, accepting the current situation. Some appear to be happier that they’re working with another high sorcerer.”

“It’s not just that. Granted, even if some of your former assembly are secretly still loyal to Thorne, they’d be overwhelmed by greater numbers. No, I’m still convinced that Thorne is trying to invent some spells of her own, which could take us completely by surprise and give her an advantage.”

“What could she be planning, though?”

“That’s what worries me, Marlys. We don’t know. Maybe she could find a way to make the ash problem worse and blame it on us. Or clear the ash safely and put herself forward as hero. Or cause you to fail and assert that you were incompetent all along and claim the high sorcerership. We haven’t had a sorcerous war in centuries, yes, but power struggles where one high sorcerer supplanted another...I read of such accounts in the journals along the Spell Passage."

"So did I," Marlys said, "but I feel we can deal with the situation. We have the advantage, after all, with six Librarians and a number of supporters among sorcerers, apprentices, and citizens."

"Still, the element of surprise has caused many a weaker sorcerer to succeed."

Marlys nodded. "I know. But there's little else we can do. I couldn't kill her if I wanted to, and I don't. Imprisoning her would make me look like a tyrant." She put a hand on Serena's shoulder. "Nonetheless, I agree that we all need to remain alert."

"That I can give my oath on," Serena said.

The next morning, Marlys awakened to see snow falling again. *So soon?* she thought. On the other hand, she did have memories of snow falling within a day or two after a previous snowfall. She hoped it would not be a pattern for the entire winter.

After rising, she walked to the window and went over in her mind all the preparations she had made for the winter. Guide rails and fences at the sides of the highways had been inspected and strengthened where needed. If someone was caught out in the snow while on the road, they could follow those to a travel shelter. The shelters had been stocked with food for people and fodder for animals. Ropes or rails had been set up between farm houses and barns so that farmers could go out and milk the cows without losing their way in a blizzard. Farmers had taken their animals from distant pastures and confined them in pens close to the barns, which had been well supplied with feed and fodder. Everyone had been supplied with food and water and places to store them; those who were elderly or disabled had been given a few waycakes to supplement their meals. Residents of towns or villages had bells at their doors to ring if they needed help. Those in outlying areas had flags to raise which could be seen by sorcerers when they made regular checks in their vicinity.

Despite all that, Marlys could not help but wonder if she had missed anything. By comparing her efforts with High Sorcerers in other regions, she found that others had made similar preparations. Still, unexpected events were inevitable. All she could do was rely on herself and her allies to meet challenges as they came up. Certainly, Goldenvalley had no lack of magical talent.

At breakfast, the apprentices hurriedly took their dishes to the kitchen after finishing their meals. When they emerged, Celestine rose from her seat.

"Wait," she called. "Where do you think you're going?"

"Sledding, Sorcerer Celestine," one said shyly.

"Not until after those on kitchen duty have completed their tasks, and not until after we've had morning lessons," Celestine said.

Marlys noticed the downcast faces. "We excused you yesterday, but we're not excusing you for the rest of the winter. You can still go sledding, but you need to attend to your chores and your studies first." She heard murmurs of "Yes, High Sorcerer Marlys" in reply, and added, "You all want to be sorcerers some day, don't you?"

The faces brightened slightly.

"Then you need to learn to postpone fun until after necessary duties are completed, just as the rest of us did."

"Yes, High Sorcerer Marlys." The voices were a little louder this time, the faces a little brighter. They separated to attend to their tasks.

After the morning lesson, the midday meal, and the cleanup, the apprentices excitedly grabbed their winter gear and toboggans and rushed outside. Marlys and Celestine went into the kitchen, filled a teapot, and arranged teacups on a tray. They carried them into the dining hall, where Marlys sounded the whistle to signal a gathering.

All the sorcerers arrived, including Thorne, and sat together. They passed around the cups and teapot.

"I thought it would be useful for us to go over our winter preparations," Marlys said.

The discussion that followed reassured Marlys that everything in the region that needed to be done, had been done. The sorcerers at the fortress had completed their tasks in the fortress area, and the training centers within the region had finished their preparations in their respective areas, confirming this through the sorcerous channels. Thorne followed the exchange with an expression of great interest, and said nothing until Rochelle reported the completion of one of her tasks.

"The reserves are secure," Rochelle said, "the food within is fresh, and we've distributed about ten percent among the citizens of Goldenvalley, as you instructed. The magistrates and citizens send their thanks."

"What!" Throne swung her head from Rochelle to Marlys. "You opened the reserves? At this early date? That's irresponsible!"

"Not if we have a sustained blizzard and people are confined to their homes for days," Marlys said.

"If that happens, they can ration what they have," Thorne said. "People do that all the time in a harsh winter. It's been done for centuries. My family did it when I was a child."

"So did mine," Tir said. "But in my community, there were people who were weaker for it. Some became sick due to lack of food."

"They recovered when the emergency was over, didn't they?" Thorne said.

"Most," Tir said. "Not all."

"There are casualties every winter," Thorne said. "People who use shovels and garden tools to move snow when they shouldn't and their hearts give out, that sort of thing. I can't see that this can be prevented."

Tir looked Thorne straight in the eye. "Tell you what," he said. "If we run short, we'll ration your food. Oh, I forgot, you have your own store of delicious almost-waycakes stored somewhere. So you have reserves the same as everyone else we supplied."

"I would add that we aren't the only region who has drawn on reserves," Marlys said. "Lindra at Cloverdell, Niquelle at Silvervale, and Ware at Woodlands also distributed ten percent of their reserves."

"That others performed an action doesn't mean the action is sound," Thorne said.

"No," Marlys said, "but in this case, it does mean that we're being careful to avoid unnecessary suffering."

"It doesn't mean you'll decrease the number of deaths, however," Thorne said, "especially if the reserves run out and there is no food. Then everyone dies."

"We'll have plenty of warning to take preventive measures before that happens," Marlys said.

Thorne shook her head.

"Speaking of distribution," Serena said to Marlys. "The elderly and disabled citizens were happy to get the waycakes we parceled out. We explained what they were and how to best make use of them."

"Waycakes," Thorne scoffed. "Oh, yes, one waycake is supposed to be a meal. You watch. They won't limit themselves to one. They'll gobble them up all at once and where's their reserve then?"

Tir indicated his fellow Librarians. "We all ate waycakes on our way to the Library of Sorcery when we ran out of food and none of us was even tempted to eat more than one. My hunger was more than satisfied and I did not crave any more until the next mealtime."

The other Librarians nodded or turned their attention to Thorne to confirm what Tir had said.

"You know people who keep eating food after they're satisfied," Thorne said.

"Some will, no doubt," Marlys said. "But most won't, and even if most use the waycakes properly, I would consider that a success."

Celestine poured herself another cup of tea. "My grandmother made us seedcakes to last us through the winter. In harsh winters, there were days when we might have one seedcake a day. These were not waycakes, but they were satisfying. My brother and I sometimes broke off a piece of each of ours and saved it so that we would have something to eat later in the day."

Marlys heard a thump against the window. She turned and saw a snowball sliding down from the pane. Outside, the snow, which had floated down lightly in the morning, now fell so thickly they could not see as far as the nearest tree. The wind howled as it blew the flakes around in sheets and swirls.

"The apprentices aren't back yet," Marlys said.

Astrid rushed to the glass and pressed her forehead against the pane. "They aren't near the windows."

Tir cast the spell that allowed one to see through a thick fog. "They aren't in the immediate area."

"I see you are careless with your apprentices as well," Thorne scolded. "They can't use sorcery to find their way or heat themselves. Even some who were well schooled in winter lore have died just outside their front steps in a blizzard because they could not tell where they were, or the cold was too severe, or the snow was too deep for them to go any farther. Does their welfare mean nothing to you?"

"Later, woman!" Marlys said to Thorne, as she and other sorcerers cast the locator spell at the same time.

Thorne looked as if she had been punched in the face.

Chapter 18

"Lyra's about a stone's throw away," Marlys said.

"The others are in a cluster in the fruit tree grove," Celestine said.

Marlys nodded at Celestine. "Use Nessa's end point spell to bring Lyra back." She gestured. "Rochelle, you come with me. We'll get the others."

"I'll cast that spell," Nessa said.

Just before she entered the circle, Marlys heard the other sorcerers calling for blankets, tea, and warm soup.

When Marlys emerged from the end point spell, she saw the toboggans set up to form a rough shelter. Ducking her head to go inside, she could see three apprentices holding crudely-made flares—the best they could do with household spells. All the apprentices sat on the ground, clustered together, sharing the blankets they used to pad the toboggans.

When they saw Marlys and Rochelle, they called out. "Oriana is very cold. She's falling asleep. We're trying to keep her awake."

Rochelle immediately extracted Oriana from the group, lifted her up, and carried her through the glowing circle.

"Gather your things, take the toboggans, and follow Rochelle." Marlys kindled a sorcerous light. "Put out your flares." They did. "Anyone need help walking?" Marlys heard murmured nos and saw others shake their heads. She got behind them and gently pushed them toward the glowing end point.

Once back in the dining hall, Nessa closed the circle. Lyra was already there, sitting close to Oriana. Both had warmed blankets draped over their shoulders. Rochelle bent over Oriana and spoke to her softly.

Sorcerers gathered the toboggans, placed blankets over the shoulders of the other apprentices, and led them to the tables. All were quickly supplied with steaming mugs of chicken soup.

"Can I have tea, too?" Lyra asked, and others echoed her.

"Right away," Astrid said, and disappeared into the kitchen.

Glancing around, Marlys saw Thorne standing a few steps away. When Thorne opened her mouth, Marlys pointed at her. "Later."

Thorne closed her mouth, raised her eyebrows, and said, "I was going to say that I've warmed the hall here and raised the light level."

After scanning the room to confirm this, Marlys faced Thorne and said "Thank you."

Rochelle straightened up and turned to Marlys. "Oriana says she's fine, just cold."

Marlys nodded and sat across from Lyra. "Did you throw the snowball?"

Lyra took another sip of tea before speaking. "Yes. When we had to stop because the snow was so thick we could barely move and hardly see, I recognized the pear tree we harvested in the fall. I put a small mark on the trunk to remind me I'd been there. I knew that the fortress was due east of the tree, so I used the compass household spell. I told the others to stay put and I would go get help. But I hadn't gone far when the snow got too deep and the wind got too strong for me to go farther, so I threw snowballs."

"Well done!" Tir said.

"However did you get to the orchard?" Thorne asked. "I thought you were tobogganing down the hill in front of the fortress."

That was a question Marlys wanted an answer to as well, so she stood silently as the apprentices exchanged guilty looks.

Eventually, one of them spoke softly. "The hill near the orchard is more exciting. It has bumps so the toboggan goes up and down, and grooves in the side so we can guide the toboggan in a semicircle."

"You realize," Thorne said, "that if you had stuck to the hill at the front of the fortress, you could have used the guide rail on the path to feel your way back when the snow became too thick to see where you were going."

Again, the apprentices exchanged guilty looks.

Thorne rolled her eyes and sighed.

"She's right," Marlys said, ignoring Thorne's astonished gasp. "From now on, you are not to go sledding anywhere but the hill in front of the fortress unless there's a sorcerer with you."

"But you're all so busy," squeaked one of the apprentices.

Marlys looked around. "Any sorcerer who would give up an hour or two to go sledding with the apprentices when asked, raise your hand."

Almost every hand went up. Marlys raised hers. Thorne kept hers by her side.

"Any questions?" Marlys asked.

"Do we have to do extra cleaning duty?" an apprentice said softly.

"Goodness, no," Marlys said. "We're all happy just to see you back here, safe. This was partially my fault...."

"...our fault," corrected Tir.

"...for not noticing you had been gone too long. I apologize."

"I think I can speak for the others when I say that we are sincerely sorry," Celestine said.

The other sorcerers, save Thorne, murmured agreement.

Lyra looked at her fellow apprentices. "We're sorry, too. We won't do it again."

The apprentices all mumbled some form of "sorry."

"We promise not to let it happen again, either," Marlys said. "So everyone can consider the matter settled."

Scanning the room, Marlys saw expressions of relief on nearly everybody. "Finish your mugs," Marlys said to the apprentices, and then we'll escort you to your dormitory so you can lie down for a while."

"We don't need to lie down," Lyra said.

"Yes, you do," Nessa said. "Marlys, Serena, Rochelle, and Tir rescued Zaria and I from a snowbank at the start of the Spell Passage. We found we needed the rest after all that time in the cold and snow."

"If you aren't feeling sleepy," Marlys said, "just relax for a while. You're free to sit on your beds and talk. You could even practice meditation."

"What about supper?" an apprentice asked.

"We'll wake you in time," Marlys promised.

The sorcerers escorted the apprentices to their dormitory. When they were all at their beds, Marlys stood at the door. "May the Bright Beings watch over you, always," she said, and slowly shut the door.

Esme set a chair near the doorway and sat. "I'll stay in case they need anything."

"Thank you, Esme." Marlys turned to the others. "I can use a nap myself. I'll be in my room." She slowly walked through the halls and up the stairs to her bedroom, where she sat and wept.

When Marlys had composed herself and dried her face, she looked up to see Thorne at the doorway, arms crossed in front of her chest. "We need to talk."

Marlys stood. Thorne backed up. Marlys walked out of her bedroom and into the study, where the two sorcerers planted themselves in the middle, facing each other.

"Now that we're away from the collaborators that you hold in thrall," Thorne said, "we can speak plainly."

"You can speak plainly at any time," Marlys said.

"Ha!" Thorne tossed her head. "Your lackeys think you're perfect. One can hardly get in a word edgewise with them around."

"What is it that you have to say?" Marlys asked.

"You need to step down as high sorcerer here. You are clearly incompetent. Today's events prove it."

"I have no intention of giving up my position. I made a mistake, that's all. Don't tell me you never made a mistake in your long tenure."

"Not one that resulted in a region full of graves."

"Graves? Point to them."

"Not yet, but that's where this region is heading if you continue to act as if you're the high sorcerer here."

"I am the high sorcerer here. There is no one in this fortress who would follow you if you supplanted me."

"They'd get used to it. There are ways."

"Oh, yes, force and cruelty. The hallmarks of your reign."

"Life is suffering, child. If you haven't learned that by now, you're learned nothing."

"Suffering comes to all whether they seek it out or not. The aim of life is to reduce suffering and increase kindness."

"You think me unkind? Unfeeling?"

"You have been, yes. Since I released you from the time-binding spell, I have seen occasions when I felt you might have a heart, after all."

"Oh, how generous of you," Thorne said sarcastically.

"I have given you more than enough time to come around, but I have my limits and you are getting near them."

"You have given me enough time? Child, I have given you more than enough time to see the truth."

"Truth?"

"The truth that you are entirely unsuited to be a high sorcerer."

"I've managed for twelve years without much complaint."

"Twelve years when you've had it easy. You never had any difficult challenges."

"Easy? You think it was easy to rebuild a sorcerous assembly from scratch? To undo all the damage you did, to those who cringed when sorcerers appeared, keeping silent because they feared that we'd withdraw our magical assistance."

"Fear among the populace isn't such a bad thing, which you'd realize if you had any sense. And I have no sympathy for you to have to rebuild a sorcerous assembly. You did that to yourself."

"I did, and I have long since taken responsibility for it."

Thorne snorted. "You hardly know what responsibility means."

"In your case, it means giving you a chance to redeem yourself even though you continue to try to undermine me."

"Redeem myself? From what? And what of you and your lackeys diminishing me? Shadowing me day and night. Minimizing my accomplishments. Dismissing my opinions, as you did today. And what of your 'later, woman!' as if I were a wayward apprentice. That was the ultimate in disrespect. Such insubordination to a high sorcerer has resulted in banishment."

"You're right, I shouldn't have said that. I was carried away by my concern for the apprentices. I should have known better. It would have been disrespectful to say that to anyone, regardless of their title. I apologize."

Thorne stared at Marlys a moment before replying. "There are places where you would have been forgiven for such a concession. I doubt I would."

"My apology is not dependent on your acceptance."

Taking a long breath, Thorne replied. "My point remains. You are incompetent and you should step aside."

"Even if I wanted to, I would not. I created an entire assembly whose loyalty is to me, and I would be betraying that if I stepped aside. Loyalty goes both ways."

Thorne stepped forward until their faces were merely a handspan apart. "One day you will fail, and I will be here to take your place when that day comes. I only hope that you haven't wrecked this region beyond repair."

"And one day, your rigidity will have carried you too far, and I hope when that day comes, you will have not wrecked your life beyond repair."

Thorne let out a huff. "I'm done arguing with a sorcerer who has no sense." She retired into her bedroom and shut the door behind her.

Feeling the need for a cup of tea after that exchange, Marlys left the suite and strolled into the hall, almost colliding with Rochelle.

"Sorry," Marlys said. "I didn't notice...." Looking beyond Rochelle, Marlys saw all of the sorcerers, except Esme, gathered there in the hallway.

"Were you listening all this time?" Marlys said.

Rochelle grinned. "More fun than the day Tir got his hand stuck in the honey jar."

Tir laughed. "Not even close." He turned to Marlys. "Can I be your head lackey?"

"I'd rather be a collaborator that you hold in thrall," Celestine said.

Rochelle put an arm around Marlys and said conspiratorially, "Tell me, how does it feel to be surrounded by sorcerers who think you are perfect?"

"Surround me with sorcerers who think I'm perfect and I'll tell you," Marlys said.

"Good point," Tir said.

"I'm in the mood for tea," Marlys said. "Who's with me?"

Chapter 19

The next morning, before she had a chance to get dressed, Marlys received a communication through the sorcerous channels from Voni.

"The early risers among us say that there are drifts out there that have reached the eaves of houses," Voni said.

Marlys peered out the window. "The snow seems to have stopped."

"It has," Voni said, "but I went out briefly and the snow pack reaches above my knees."

"We'll have to put all the sorcerers to work clearing snow, then," Marlys said. "Did Zaria teach everyone Thorne's snow-clearing spell?"

"Yes," Voni said, "but it seemed that some sorcerers, particularly older ones like Elspeth, already knew it."

"I wouldn't expect that Thorne would be the only one to know such a spell."

"I'll leave you to your work, then." Voni closed the channel.

When they were all at breakfast, Marlys raised her voice. "The snow is thick enough so that all of the sorcerers here need to go out, clear the roads and paths, and check on those in remote areas." She turned to the apprentices. "All of you apprentices need to stay here, and by that I mean stay inside until we return. Can I rely on you to do that?"

She saw nods in reply. A few said, "Yes, High Sorcerer Marlys" in soft voices.

Marlys turned to Lyra. "Lyra, you're the senior apprentice. I'm counting on you to remind the others if they forget."

"Yes, High Sorcerer Marlys." Lyra said.

"We won't forget," added Oriana.

Marlys smiled. "Good."

After they finished eating, the apprentices all rose from their seats. "We can clean up while you go out and work."

"Thank you," Marlys said.

Thorne stood. "I'm going, too."

Marlys turned to her. "With your experience in clearing snow, your help will be most welcome."

Thorne sighed and shrugged as the other sorcerers pushed their chairs back.

A permanent map of Goldenvalley had been painted and preserved on a wall in the audience room. While the sorcerers donned coats and jackets, Marlys assigned each of them an area in the vicinity of the fortress. Then they all quickly moved outside. The Librarians cast their transportation spell. The others cast the end point spell.

As Marlys cleared roads, she checked farmsteads and cottages along the way. Many had placed flags outside their windows, since drifts had not allowed them to open the doors. Farmers thanked Marlys for clearing the way so they could milk their cows. Since most farm animals had already been gathered into barns and pens and coops, only a few had been lost. In those cases, Marlys helped prepare the meat for outdoor freezing and storage for later use.

In the villages and towns, Marlys cleared the roads and paths to doors, also blocked by drifts. Outside the towns, she came across a family in one of the travel shelters, glad they could continue on their journey after Marlys removed snow from the main thoroughfare.

When she finished, Marlys returned to the fortress. Inside, she was met by the apprentices, emerging from the kitchen. All wore aprons which covered them from neck to knee, and a few had dabs of flour on their faces.

"Am I the first to return?" Marlys asked.

"Yes," Lyra said.

"You're been cooking?"

The apprentices smiled. "I showed them how to make waycakes," Lyra said humbly.

"Oh? What were the results?"

Lyra gestured to her companions. "We had a few not come out exactly, though they were still good. But a couple of batches were genuine waycakes. They tasted the same as the ones we made with Brianna."

"You did very well," Marlys said. "I'm proud of you."

"We were just cleaning up when you came," Oriana said.

"By all means, return to your cleaning," Marlys said.

They returned to the kitchen.

Marlys sensed motion by her side and turned to see Thorne coming out of a circle of light. She started to take off her jacket, and seeing Marlys, said, "No casualties along my route. The citizens of Goldenvalley seemed to have the Bright Beings watching over them this time, and have not forgotten their winter sense. I came across a man who had not made it to a travel shed and simply waited out the storm in a crude shelter he made under a tree put using piled snow and branches."

"The apprentices made their own shelter yesterday from the toboggans," Marlys said.

"Yes, most of us were taught young about what to do," Thorne said. "It doesn't guarantee survival, but it often makes for a better outcome."

The remainder of the sorcerers began to come in. All reported that they found no casualties due to the storm.

"They all seemed well prepared," Tir said as he removed a snow-crusted jacket.

"I see we returned just in time for the midday meal," Celestine said.

Marlys gestured to the kitchen door. "Lyra taught the apprentices how to make waycakes in our absence."

"Well done," Tir said. "Were they any good?"

"Lyra said that they were all good," Marlys said, "and some were genuine waycakes."

Serena waved at Rochelle. "Since Rochelle and I are currently on kitchen duty, we may as well join them and get started."

As they ate the midday meal, Astrid called out to the apprentices. "Since you all did excellent work while we were away, I'll help Serena and Rochelle with the cleanup."

"I will, too," Esme said.

"Then we can have an afternoon lesson to make up for the lack of a morning lesson," Celestine said.

Marlys saw eager faces among the apprentices. Lessons meant learning spells and everything else they needed to know to become sorcerers!

The room that they used for teaching apprentices had a door which opened out to the dining hall. Marlys lingered at the open doorway, contributing to Celestine's instruction from time to time. She also watched Thorne, who had remained in the dining hall with a cup of tea and some of the near-waycakes, reading a book of ancient tales Serena had placed in the fortress's library.

Meanwhile, in the classroom, Celestine reviewed yesterday's lesson and demonstration of the sorcerous channel spell. The apprentices listened attentively.

Celestine concluded by saying, "That's the reason that we want you to go sledding with a sorcerer from now on. If you get lost or injured, the sorcerer can use the channels to contact the rest of us for help immediately."

"Speaking of which," Marlys added, "I wanted to commend all of you for doing what you needed to do when confronted with an unexpected event. You used your toboggans to shelter you against the wind, you huddled together for warmth, you used your household spells to kindle flares, and when one of you was in distress, you stayed together and sent the one who had the plan and used the appropriate household spell to get help. Being a sorcerer is not just about casting spells. Sorcerers also need to use all of their knowledge and common sense to deal with complicated situations. From what I saw yesterday, I can tell you will all become exceptional sorcerers."

Marlys saw grins all around.

"Now, for today's lesson," Celestine said, drawing their attention again, "I'm going to explain the time-binding spell."

"But Sorcerer Celestine," Lyra said, "we were all pledged not to use it."

"...on each other," Celestine said. "You can use it on anyone not in Goldenvalley's assembly."

"I first used it on a bear in the woods," Marlys added.

"Whether we can actually use it right now or not, I can still explain the spell," Celestine said, and did.

"I have a question," Lyra said. "We all swore not to use the time-binding spell on each other. What happens if we try?"

"Good question." Celestine turned to Marlys. "Watch what happens when I try to time-bind Marlys."

Marlys stepped forward and spread her arms.

Celestine cast the spell, or at least, tried to.

Marlys put her arms down. “See? The spell failed.”

Oriana scooted forward a little on her chair. “What about the spell that prevents sorcerers from hurting each other?”

“You know how you might accidentally bump into each other, or step on another’s foot?” Celestine asked.

The apprentices all nodded.

“I don’t know whether you’ve noticed,” Celestine said, “but we don’t do that.”

Marlys stepped close to Celestine. “Watch.” With Celestine facing her, smiling, Marlys made a move as if to slap Celestine in the face. Marlys missed.

Celestine tried to slap Marlys. She missed.

Marlys motioned to Lyra. “Come over.”

Lyra scrambled out of her chair and stood by Marlys.

“Now,” Marlys said, “step on my foot. Not too hard, but step on it.”

Lyra did.

“Thank you, Lyra. Celestine?” Marlys said.

Celestine tried to step on Marlys’s foot. She missed.

The apprentices made noises of delight.

Oriana looked at the other apprentices. “We’re going to have to watch the sorcerers more closely.”

Lyra returned to her seat. “What would happen if a sorcerer tried really hard to hurt another sorcerer?”

“When Thorne administered the oath to me, she said my life would be forfeit,” Marlys said.

“Do you know of anyone who tried it and died?” Oriana asked.

Marlys took a moment to think. She shook her head and turned to Celestine, who shrugged.

Looking through the doorway to the dining hall, Marlys saw Thorne still reading and sipping tea. “We could ask Thorne. She’s been around a long time.”

“Aren’t we supposed to avoid talking to Thorne?” Oriana said in a stage whisper.

“It’s best if we sorcerers did the talking to her,” Marlys said, “but it’s not forbidden. Just use caution.” She stepped to the doorway and called, “Thorne?”

Thorne looked up.

"When you administered the oath to me not to harm another sorcerer, you said my life would be forfeit, is that right?"

Thorne put the book down, took her teacup, and stood. "Why? Are you thinking of striking another sorcerer?"

Marlys inclined her head toward the classroom. "We wanted to know if you knew of any cases where a sorcerer tried it, and died."

Teacup in hand, Thorne walked over. At the same time, Marlys saw Rochelle and Serena emerge from the kitchen.

When Thorne reached the doorway, drawing even with Marlys, she stopped. She looked inside the classroom but did not enter. "I've heard of a case, a very long time ago, when two sorcerers who hated each other tried to push past the spell. Both died, yes."

By this time, Rochelle and Serena reached the doorway. They stood about a step behind Thorne, but still had a clear view of the inside of the classroom. The apprentices turned to them with expressions of interest.

"At my first training center, southwest of here," Rochelle said, "they told us apprentices the story of Ineth and Primari."

Thorne inhaled sharply and turned to Rochelle. "Yes, those were the names!"

Rochelle leaned forward a little. "What they said was that Ineth and Primari were apprentices at that very training center. Friends at first, but as time went on, and particularly after both became sorcerers, the friendship dissolved into bitter rivalry. Each thought the other performed spells clumsily, that sort of thing. The other sorcerers did their best to quell their arguments. There were periods of peace followed by heated quarrels. The High Sorcerer separated them, assigning them to distant training centers. Still, somehow, they found their paths crossing. Finally, fed up with their constant bickering, they were banished...not only from the region, but from all regions."

"The other High Sorcerers didn't want them, either?" Celestine guessed.

Rochelle nodded. "They had a reputation. Both were angry at being exiled. Their only choice was to go to an area of the continent entirely unknown to them, and that made them more furious. They blamed each other. But they had to leave. Even the citizens wanted them out. The local magistrate escorted them beyond the borders of the region and stood by watching them walk down the road to make sure they left."

"Arguing all the way, I would guess," Marlys said.

"Precisely," Rochelle said. "While the magistrate watched, they left the road and stood in a meadow, facing each other. The magistrate felt an energy, and wasn't sure whether he should run or stay and watch. He realized they were casting spells. The very air vibrated. Then suddenly, BOOM! The ground shook. Debris soared into the air. The magistrate was pushed to the ground as if there were a sudden wind. When the air cleared, the magistrate could not see either sorcerer. He rose and walked to the meadow where he found a crater. There were nothing left to bury but a few charred teeth and pieces of jewelry they wore. When that was done, the High Sorcerer of the region at the time had a stone marker made to set there. As a warning, my sorcerer-trainer said. She took all of us apprentices to see the marker, and said that was a reminder to take the oath not to harm another sorcerer seriously."

Thorne turned to Marlys. "To answer your question, that's what I meant when I said your life would be forfeit if you harmed another sorcerer."

"I took that warning seriously, believe me," Marlys said.

"I think I know of another case," Serena said.

Everyone gave Serena their full attention.

"As you know, I stopped at quite a few training centers between Majesticacres and here to become a sorcerer. At one of them, I heard a story of a sorcerer gone rogue. Bad temper. Wouldn't accept correction, did whatever she wanted with increasing ferocity. Wrecked houses of those who offended her, and she took offense easily. Said they deserved it. When she nearly killed a citizen, and would have if there hadn't been another sorcerer nearby to give an immediate healing, they'd had enough. The sorcerers at the training center came together and tried to push her through a portal to the island worlds. She resisted and almost dragged the others in. To keep her from doing that, the High Sorcerer attacked her. She retaliated, and they pushed back against their oath not to harm each other fiercely. The vicious battle ended when the rogue sorcerer died. The other sorcerers thought that the High Sorcerer died, too, but found she still had breath in her, so they did their best to heal her. But she was never the same. She could no longer cast sorcerous spells. Weak household spells she could do only with difficulty. She was bedridden for the rest of her life, which only lasted a few years more, though she was far from elderly."

"Strange that this story is not more widely known," Celestine said.

"Those telling the story said that it took place so long ago they wondered if it were a mere fable to make the point that one should not assault other sorcerers."

"Or should not become a rogue," Celestine added.

"There's a lot of knowledge that has been lost or unshared," Marlys said. "We found that out on the Spell Passage, and especially at the Library of Sorcery."

"I agree this is a matter that needs more attention," Serena said.

"Apprentices, in particular, need to know the possible consequences of their actions," Thorne said, throwing the apprentices inside the classroom a meaningful look.

Marlys noticed the apprentices turning from Thorne to her with *We don't know quite what to say to that* expressions. "I can assure you," Marlys said to Thorne, "that all of us here have given these stories our utmost attention."

Chapter 20

Marlys felt relieved when two more days without snow went by. With no word from the Library of Sorcery, she contacted Genevieve.

"Can you be ready tomorrow?" Genevieve asked.

"Yes. I wondered if we might meet," Marlys said.

"I can give instructions about our next steps through the sorcerous channels," Genevieve said.

"This is for another matter," Marlys said. "I, too, have been thinking of what other spells we might use to clear the ash. I wondered if the sorcerous weapons at Overlook might be of any help."

"Sorcerous weapons? At Overlook?" Genevieve said.

"Yes, along the Spell Passage. Didn't you know about them?" Marlys said.

"No," Genevieve said. "I didn't think any sorcerous weapons existed anywhere but here."

"They're at Overlook. I saw them," Marlys said.

"We need to make a visit. Right away," Genevieve said.

Marlys contacted Kayli through the sorcerous channels. She met Genevieve and Marlys as they emerged from their respective transportation spells at the tower.

"I'm glad that you're working on ways to disperse the ash," Kayli said. "Having snows this deep all winter would be disastrous."

Genevieve nodded. "We agree. The snows have fallen throughout the continent. Can you show me the weapons?"

Using the climbing spell, they all reached the top of the tower. Once inside, Genevieve quickly looked around.

"We couldn't even touch the weapons," Marlys said.

"The only ones we can handle use house minor spells, such as this orb here," Kayli said.

Genevieve walked over to the central round table and touched the orb. "This tells whether someone is being deceitful, so it is of use."

"You know of it, then," Marlys said.

"Yes, we have one at the Library." Genevieve strolled around looking at the weapons and artifacts against the wall. She reached out to touch them, but her hand met a barrier each time.

"Do you recognize these?" Marlys asked. "Do you know what these are used for?"

Genevieve shook her head. "I'm sorry to say I have no idea." She turned to Kayli. "Do you have any written instructions here for these?"

"No," Kayli said. "Not even their names. We certainly don't know how to use them. All we have are writings that say when they are needed, we'll be able to reach them."

Genevieve sighed. "That kind of spell."

"What kind of spell?" Marlys asked, curious.

"After the sorcerous wars, the survivors, the victors, locked away a number of artifacts. We have some in the forbidden vault that you saw, Marlys. They set the conditions upon which the unlocking would take place, but made no record of those, fearing that someone might cause the events to happen in order to use the artifacts to start another war. But, if whatever circumstances they set are met, we'll be able to lay hands on them. The weapons will tell us, somehow, how to use them."

"Frustrating," Kayli said.

"You aren't the first to make that observation," Genevieve said.

"I take it then, that since we can't touch them, they'd be no use to us in the present situation," Marlys said.

"Unfortunately not," Genevieve said. "But I'm glad I know they're here, nonetheless. We try to keep track of them."

When Marlys returned to Goldenvalley, Tir and Serena met her in the audience room.

"Any luck?" Tir asked.

"No," Marlys said. "The weapons at Overlook won't help us."

"At least you tried," Serena said. "I thought it would be best to tell you that Tir and Rochelle and I have observed Thorne testing out spells. She's definitely trying to develop new spells."

"Spells that we would then know nothing about and may not be able to counter right away," Tir said.

"Any clues as to what she's aiming for?" Marlys said.

"She seems to be concentrating on two spells in particular. One is a variation of Nessa's end point spell, which is a variation of the distance shortening spell."

Marlys considered that for a moment. "She can't be thinking of duplicating the transportation spell, which would be the logical next step. She hasn't the power."

"An escape spell is what we're thinking," Serena said.

"That would make sense," Marlys said. "Since confining her is something we still might do, and she knows it."

"If it's something that could defeat the locator spell," Tir said, "this would be a problem."

Marlys nodded. "What's the other spell?"

"A whirlwind spell," Serena said.

Marlys's eyebrows furrowed. "A whirlwind spell? Where would that take her? Every child I know who could do household spells has amused themselves at some point conjuring little dust devils, but it never went beyond that. What would be the use, except if she managed to conjure a tornado, and all that would do is destroy a lot of land and houses and crops and people. Thorne may have a cruel streak, but she knows that destroying food and workers won't do her any good."

"When I was at the Library of Sorcery," Tir said, "I read of a whirlwind spell that would do just that...create a tornado, or something like it. The sorcerer who recorded the spell noted that this spell seemed to have no useful purpose, either, but recorded it simply to make one aware that it could be done."

"We know how to counter a tornado anyway," Serena said. "The problem with tornados is that a sorcerer has to be within sight of one to do anything about it. Most of the time, by the time we hear of it, it has already done its damage and is gone."

While they were talking, Rochelle entered the room. "She could use it as a weapon against us, throw it at us."

"But that would violate the oath not to do another sorcerer harm," Marlys said.

"She could use one to distract us while making some other sort of mischief," Rochelle said.

Marlys let out a breath. "We'll just have to keep watching her. We can't stop her from trying out spells, and who knows? She may fail."

"A sorcerer of her experience?" Serena said. "I wouldn't count on it."

"That's why we have to keep watching her," Marlys said. "Thank you all for staying alert."

The next day, Genevieve used the sorcerous channels to tell Marlys and the other Librarians at Goldenvalley where to position themselves to use the ash clearing spell. Marlys remained at Goldenvalley as the other Librarians moved to other places within the continent.

As she cast the spell and sustained it, she noticed Thorne observing her intently, saying nothing. When the spell had done its work, Thorne silently returned to the fortress.

The day after that, another blizzard smothered the area with snow. No one could go out until the next morning. After that, they were busy clearing snow.

Upon returning to the fortress, Celestine reported that in one of the villages where she had cleared snow, the magistrate reported that a man had been caught out in the storm and died. All of them found more frozen animals. Astrid reported that a storage shed—not the reserve storage house the sorcerers maintained, but a private storehouse—had burned. The steward had forgotten to snuff out a candle when visiting it, and due to the storm, no one noticed until the snowfall had stopped.

"There wasn't much left to salvage," Astrid said.

"In the area I was in, a warming fire got out of control," Tir reported. "No casualties, but I had to resettle a family into another shelter."

Throne turned to Marlys. "Seems that your plan to clear the ash isn't working so well. Things are getting worse. And now we have even less food to share than before."

Marlys faced her. "Then what would you do?"

"Rationing is the least you should do," Thorne said. "If we don't do it now, there'll be nothing by the end of winter."

"Magistrates I visited were not concerned about that," Serena said. "They were concerned about the snow. We are clearing roads and clearing roofs so they don't collapse. However, the sheer volume and weight of the snow everywhere could create problems later."

"The winter wheat had been sewn," Tir said. "It may survive."

"And it may not," Thorne said. "More food shortages."

"In speaking to other high sorcerers and the Library of Sorcery, none of us think that rationing is something we need to do at this time," Marlys said. "Though none of us is ruling it out as a future option."

Thorne huffed, turned on her heel, and stomped off.

The next day brought no snow, though the sky remained overcast. After breakfast and the morning lesson, Esme accompanied the apprentices on a tobogganing run. Marlys crossed the audience room on the way to the kitchen for tea and found Tir lying on the floor, looking out the window.

"What is she doing?" Tir murmured to himself.

Marlys strolled over, craned her head, and looked out the window. Thorne stood by herself in an area largely cleared of snow—it was so deep now that it was impossible to walk anywhere except paths or patches of ground that had been cleared of snow. Marlys saw what seemed to be snow swirls rising upward beyond the treetops.

Marlys turned to Tir. "Creating a display?"

Without lifting his head, Tir gestured with his hand. "There seems to be a pattern, I don't know what. From my vantage point here, I can see lightning sprites and what seems to be a spiral column of snowflakes ascending to the clouds." He sat and regarded Marlys. "You and Serena are better than me at learning spells by observing and analyzing what other sorcerers do. What do you think?"

Marlys watched Thorne a while longer while Tir rose and joined her at the window. "I need a closer look."

"Do we dare go out?" Tir asked. "Will she stop? That would defeat our purpose in trying to determine what she's doing."

"I can't learn any more from here," Marlys said. "We'll have to risk it, I think." She heard footsteps and turned to see Serena. "Serena, Tir and I are going outside to see if we can tell what Thorne's up to."

Serena glanced out the window and nodded. "Thorne seems very absorbed in her work. I think if we are quiet about it, and approach from behind, it may be a while before she notices us."

"Stealthy is something I can do," Tir said.

Using their best camouflage spells, they left the fortress and gently parted the snow to reach a point within a few paces behind Thorne.

From what Marlys could see, Thorne appeared to be attempting a variation of the "touch the sky" spell. This was a spell that many new sorcerers cast to amuse themselves. One would try to throw something upward to see how far it would rise. Occasionally, sorcerers would stage an informal contest to see who could compel sand or autumn leaves to travel the farthest. Tir had been particularly adept at this spell, and would sometimes entertain an audience of sorcerers and apprentices by adding lightning sprites for effect.

Thorne gathered and used the snow surrounding her, making it spiral upward using a vortex spell to give it height. Marlys was impressed at how far upward Thorne could cast the snowflakes.

Eventually, Thorne lowered her arms. Her shoulders sagged as she took a couple of deep breaths. Taking a rest, Marlys thought.

Tir canceled his camouflage spell and stepped toward Thorne. "Good, but I have some questions."

Thorne gasped and turned around.

Marlys and Serena dropped their camouflage spells and walked over.

Tir ignored Thorne's scowl and said, "Very impressive. I admire your technique at casting a wide spiral which spins more rapidly as you narrow it. That seems to give it more strength and reach."

"I'm not interested in teaching this, especially to those who are spying on me." Her glare took in Marlys and Serena as well.

"Granted," Tir said, undaunted. "But I think I have it." He turned to Marlys and Serena. "See if this seems to capture the essence of the spell." Tir looked up, raised his arms, swept them downward to gather snow, and then cast the spell upward.

Marlys followed the snow funnel as Tir shaped it from a wide spiral to a narrow one. The snowflakes gained speed and rose quickly, forcefully. Glancing to one side, she saw Thorne giving Tir and his spell her full attention.

Without taking his eyes from the rising snowflake spiral, Tir said, "That's it, isn't it?

Thorne turned her attention from the sky to Tir, but said nothing.

Tir faced Thorne briefly. When he received no response, he gazed skyward again. "Let me try to improve on this." He gathered more snowflakes, and hoisted them into the air again, starting with a wide spiral that he narrowed as the snow flakes rose.

Marlys watched the ascent. "I can see that you've stirred the ash, too, Tir."

Still looking up, Tir said, "Yes, I noticed it, too."

Serena stepped forward. "Let me try." She cast the spell upward, and this time the ash swirled around even more, clumping a little as it did.

Thorne shook her head. "That's not what I was aiming for. It was this." She gathered her strength and cast her spell upwards. Her feet nearly left the ground as she did so.

Feeling suddenly inspired, Marlys gathered herself as Thorne's spiral rose, and threw a variation of the Library's spell upward with all her strength. She did not pulverize the ash, nor did she try to bring it down. Instead she pushed with all her might, boosting Thorne's spell.

They all searched the air above to see the effect. For an instant, Marlys spotted a patch of blue sky.

Chapter 21

Marlys continued to gaze upward, wondering if she really saw blue sky or simply imagined it. Because the blue patch was only a dot, and lasted the barest fraction of a moment, it could have been merely an afterimage.

"You ruined my spell!" Thorne shouted.

Turning her attention to Thorne, Marlys said. "What? Ruined?"

"I almost had it! The sky almost cleared!"

Marlys took that as confirmation that it was not simply her imagination.

"A spot the length of an arm is not 'almost cleared,'" Serena said.

Thorne pointed to Marlys. "I would have if she hadn't interfered."

"Then do it again." Tir crossed his arms over his chest. "We'll wait."

Thorne cast the spell again while Marlys, Serena, and Tir stepped back to observe. No blue appeared. Repeatedly, Thorne tried with increasing force to duplicate the spell. Nothing happened. She put her arms down.

"What you probably did," Serena said, "is part the ash for an instant. It quickly filled the space again."

"At least I'm trying," Thorne said. "My spell almost worked. All you're doing is spreading ash around. I wouldn't be surprised if those Library of Sorcery spells were causing the heavy snowfalls."

"The Librarians told us that it might take until spring to see any real difference," Serena said. "They also predicted a harsh winter. None of this was unexpected."

Thorne grabbed a handful of snow and threw it forcefully to one side. Grimacing, she stalked back to the fortress, slamming the door behind her.

Tir looked from Serena to Marlys. "This may be dangerous to admit, but I think she's on to something."

"Perhaps," Serena said, "but I don't think it was her spell, or, more precisely, her spell alone. Combining spells can have powerful effects, and Marlys adding hers could have made the difference."

"You're right that a blue spot is not the same as dispersing all the ash," Marlys said.

"True." Serena said, "Though I agree with Tir that this could be a start to a genuine solution. When we were at the Library, I consulted with Genevieve about spells that I came across in hidden compartments of books."

Tir's face broke out in a smile. "You never told us about this!"

"I hadn't because they were hidden for a reason," Serena said. "These were spells that someone such as Thorne could put to ill use. However, I can think of one or two which might help us with this crisis."

"Since you say Thorne could use them, I take it that those were spells that any sorcerer could use," Marlys said.

Serena nodded.

"And weren't world-destroying spells," Tir added.

"Also true," Serena said.

Marlys took a step toward Serena. "Your experience with how to find hidden compartments has certainly aided us."

Tir grinned. "Though I can't help feeling the rest of us are missing out."

"We all have our unique talents," Marlys said. "Genevieve took me aside and told me about spells that were passed from one leading sorcerer to another. She told me those spells had been considered too likely to be abused if written and discovered."

"That risks the chain being broken if a sorcerer forgets to pass them on," Tir said, "or hoards the spells."

"These were spells that Genevieve said that any sorcerer could stumble upon but would be difficult to counter without knowing the sorcerous remedies," Marlys said.

"I see," Serena said, "if the remedies were known, it would be easy to develop the spell the remedy had been made to counter."

Tir chuckled. "This is getting complicated. I think I'll stick with more generalized spells."

Serena turned to him. "Would you be willing to get together with me and discuss what we could do with Thorne's spell? I gather you have ideas, too."

"I do," Tir said. "Marlys, do you wish to join us?"

"My concentration at the moment is keeping Thorne from mischief and this region from disaster," Marlys said. "I would only distract you. Besides, I have no ideas on how to improve on the spells at the moment. I will tell you if I do."

"Fair enough," Tir said.

Marlys did not see Tir, or Serena, or Thorne for that matter, until the midday meal. When Rochelle entered, she nodded at Marlys, indicating she had taken over monitoring Thorne for the moment.

When the meal was over, Genevieve's image appeared in the dining hall. "Marlys, I need you and the other Librarians there to come to the Library of Sorcery. Is there any reason you cannot come now?"

Marlys searched the faces of the other Librarians and saw no one objecting. "We can come, but give us a moment first."

"I look forward to seeing you soon." Genevieve's image faded.

Thorne had already left the room.

Marlys walked over to Celestine. "Can you handle the monitoring of Thorne while we're gone?"

"Of course," Celestine said.

Marlys waved the other Librarians over. "Let's go, then."

Marlys and the others emerged from the transportation spell into the audience room of the Library of Sorcery. When they all had been there earlier, they had seen only Genevieve and Blair. Now they saw what appeared to be the entire assembly of sorcerers in the Library district, as well as a number of apprentices. Marlys noticed a number of different ages, heights, weights, skin tones, hair colors, and hair styles. Tir and Blair, however, were the only men. All sat at tables, turning to Marlys and her companions with expressions of interest.

Genevieve rose from her seat. "Welcome back." She faced the assembly and introduced Marlys and the others. Both groups exchanged greetings. Genevieve gestured to empty chairs, inviting Marlys and her companions to sit.

When Genevieve had settled back into a chair, she said, "There's a spell in the room which allows everyone to hear clearly what anyone says in a normal tone of voice."

"A very useful spell!" Tir said.

"We've had a conference here and wanted to tell you the results," Genevieve said.

"Why not just use the sorcerous channels?" Marlys said.

"Our conclusion was disturbing," Genevieve said, "and we wanted all the Librarians to discuss the implications."

"What was disturbing?" Tir asked.

Genevieve gestured to a table nearby. "Our skywatchers believe that the spells we have been using to dispel the ash have been causing the blizzards."

Marlys, Serena, and Tir met each other's eyes.

"You suspected?" Genevieve said.

Marlys faced her. "The thought had been aired."

Genevieve scratched her temple. "Did you think of sharing that thought with us?"

"It was just a suspicion," Marlys said, "and only voiced a brief time before coming here."

"We still think the spell is working, nonetheless," Genevieve said. "But slowly."

"Are you still resolved to move forward despite the blizzards?" Marlys asked.

"We are uncertain whether to move forward or try other spells," Genevieve said. "There is no consensus among us."

"Do you have any other spells in mind?" Serena asked.

"Not at present," Genevieve said. "We wanted to consult with you and ask whether you wanted to continue with the spells we had or try something else."

"As a matter of fact," Tir said. "We do want to try something else."

"Tir and I have been talking about a new spell," Serena said, "or rather, a combination of spells."

"I will add that our first attempts gave us a glimpse of blue sky," Marlys said.

Many in the room gasped.

"What did you do?" a sorcerer at the skywatcher's table asked.

"This is Hailey," Genevieve said by way of introduction.

"A whirlwind spell," Tir said, "a 'touch the sky' spell, combined with Marlys using a variation of your ash dispersal spell."

"Can you demonstrate it?" Hailey asked.

"Before we do that," Tir said, "allow me to make use of your knowledge. In school, we were taught that the world is surrounded by a blanket of air, and beyond that, there is a void where the sun, moon, and other planets move."

Hailey nodded. "And some of those planets have a blanket of air as well."

"But there's nothing in the void," Tir said, "I mean, the void between all those spheres."

"Nothing of consequence that we can tell, anyway," Hailey said.

Serena leaned forward slightly. "What Tir and I have thought is that we can use a variation of the whirlwind spell to gather the ash in the upper air, guide the ash to a vortex, and then push it out into the void."

Many in the room turned to each other. They spoke in voices too low for the broadcast spell to pick up, so Marlys could not make out what was being said.

"None of us has the power to push anything that far," Genevieve said. "We've tried...unless you have found a way we know nothing about."

Tir turned and gestured at Nessa. "You know about Nessa's end point spell. What we propose is that we cast that spell so that the entry is at the level of the ash, and the exit is in the void."

"Then we gather the ash with the vortex spell and push the ash through the end point," Serena said.

"Air would go out with it," Hailey said.

"But the air is thin at that level, isn't it?" Tir said. "The air is sparse even at this level of the Shadowmount. You have spells to replenish the air here because of that."

"True," Hailey said, "but how much would we lose if we tried this?"

"With the air being even thinner at the level of the ash," Tir said, "we don't think we would lose much."

"The vortex may be weaker as well," Hailey said.

"But the vortex is powered by magic as well as air," Serena said.

“We don’t think it would take long to gather a significant amount of ash and push it through,” Tir said. “That would also minimize the loss of air.”

Again, Marlys heard low murmurs. Genevieve moved next to Hailey and had a brief whispered conference.

When she moved back, she turned to Marlys. “Can you give us a demonstration?”

The entire company moved outdoors. A few of the sorcerers cast a spell of warmth over the area. The Library grounds had been largely cleared of snow, so Marlys found it easy to walk there.

Tir raised his voice. “Cast a far-seeing spell so that you can watch. Apprentices, look up. You should be able to see something.”

Marlys saw some of the apprentices bring out spyglasses.

As everyone watched, Serena cast the end point spell. Marlys saw a bright, spinning circle at the level of the ash. At the same time, Tir created a vortex in the upper air, which swept the ash into it. He moved the vortex toward the end point.

The disturbance in the air, however, caused currents moving surrounding ash every which way. Marlys stepped next to Tir and Serena, looked up, and cast the spell to push the ash, but pushed it toward Tir’s vortex. As the effect became more widespread, Rochelle, Nessa, and Zaria cast spells to support the effort.

Marlys could see blue patches in the sky and heard exclamations of “Ah!” from the onlookers.

Serena played with the end point, narrowing it and extending it further, which seemed to suction the ash inside all the more.

Encouraged, the other Librarians began to join in. A river of ash flowed into the end point from all around. Blue patches spread.

When the sky had completely cleared above them, Serena closed the end point. She turned to Genevieve. “Convincing?”

Genevieve nodded. “It’s a start. Let’s see if it lasts.”

Tir turned to her. “You’re right. This small attempt won’t last. The ash will spread and fill in the gap eventually.”

“But at a thinner level than before,” Hailey said.

Blair stepped forward. “We can build on this. I think if we refine the spells, we can work more efficiently. If we can make the spells self-sustaining, we may be able to gather ash over a large region all at once."

"You mean like the lighting spell," Marlys said, "where the light spread from horizon to horizon and beyond once we got it started."

"Exactly," Blair said.

"Even if we can make the spell self-sustaining, however," Genevieve said, "we'll need a number of sorcerers at any given location to guide the air currents, at least at first."

"I agree," Marlys said, "but, fortunately, I believe the sorcerers don't necessarily have to be Librarians. One of the sorcerers at our fortress was able to create a vortex reaching to the level of the ash. With a large number of sorcerers capable of helping, it should be possible to send teams of sorcerers to clear ash in several places at once."

"But it will still take at least two Librarians to initiate the spells," Tir said.

Genevieve clapped her hands. "Then I say it's time for all of us to get together and work out how to do this."

Chapter 22

As Tir predicted, the sky became overcast again, though the process took a couple of hours. In that time, everyone remained in the main gathering room, discussing, exchanging ideas, adopting some strategies, discarding others. When they reached consensus, all walked outside.

Blair looked up and then back to his fellow sorcerers. "Again, we're just going to try this and see if the spell can reach a point where it is self-sustaining."

"Why not just let it go as far as it can?" Zaria said.

"To make sure that if something unexpected happens, we can contain it," Genevieve said.

Once again, Serena cast the end point spell, and Tir cast the vortex spell. This time, Blair joined in and manipulated the air currents to gather the greatest amount of ash.

"Now, let's see if it will self-sustain." Blair put his arms down and looked up.

Marlys saw the ash start to spread.

Genevieve extended herself to gather it. "Looks as if we still need sorcerers to give it a little guidance."

Other sorcerers joined in.

Serena continued to manipulate the end point to get the maximum ash and minimum air through. At some point, the ash accumulated outside the end point.

"Seems to be stuck." Marlys cast the ash-manipulating spell and put all of her sorcerous strength behind it. Serena let the end point stay where it was so that she could join Marlys in casting the ash-manipulating spell. The ash pulsed once, pulsed again, and then rushed entirely through the end point.

Serena then closed the end point and put her arms down, breathing hard.

"Look at the light!" Tir said.

Marlys looked up. "Yes, it's nice to see the sun again."

"No," Tir said. "I mean you and Serena."

Marlys turned to Serena. Beyond Serena's usual aura, she glowed with a yellow light. Looking down at her hands, Marlys saw that she, too, glowed.

Genevieve stepped forward with a smile and put one hand on Marlys's shoulder and one on Serena's. "You have achieved brilliance."

"Meaning?" Marlys asked.

"Meaning you have reached the pinnacle of your sorcerous powers," Blair said. "It's very rare. Genevieve has achieved it, but the rest of us are still aspiring to it."

"Are we going to be a continuous light source, then?" Serena asked.

"No," Genevieve said kindly. "You can see that I'm not. But from time to time, when you exercise your sorcerous strength, you will glow briefly. See? It's already fading to your usual aura."

Tir chuckled. "In that case, I shall start aspiring, too!"

After devising a strategy as to how to rid the air of the rest of the ash, Marlys and the other Goldenvalley Librarians used the transportation spell to get back home. They emerged in the audience hall and found all the sorcerers and apprentices gathered there.

"Is something amiss?" Marlys asked.

Celestine stepped forward. "We all need to talk to you."

Marlys looked around. "Where's Thorne?"

"Right now, she's in the fortress's library," Celestine said. "Earlier, she was practicing spells. That's what we need to discuss with you." She gestured toward the classroom.

They all crowded in. While there was room for all to stand or sit comfortably, they all were closer than they would be in a usual assembly meeting.

Celestine shut the door. "Just to be sure."

"What's this about?" Marlys said.

Celestine turned to Marlys. "While you were away, Thorne was outside, experimenting with whirlwind spells: sending them up and around. She was able to control them, but some came dangerously close to the fortress."

"She scares me," Oriana said. Other apprentices nodded.

"Marlys," Celestine said, "you have to do something about her before she causes any real damage. A sorcerer of her years and experience could do something catastrophic."

Marlys spread her hands. "What would you suggest?"

Celestine crossed her arms in front of her. "If it were up to me, I'd have sent her through the portal to the island worlds long before this. It would be just. We all saw how she tried to send you, Serena, Tir, and Rochelle through."

"If it were just Thorne we would have to worry about," Marlys said, "I might consider it."

"I can't think of anyone who wouldn't be glad to see her gone," Celestine said.

"What about the members of my old assembly?" Marlys said.

"What about them?" Astrid chimed in. "From the gossip I've gathered through the sorcerous channels, they're all satisfied with you being High Sorcerer instead of her."

"Yes," Marlys said, "but that's because of how I've dealt with Thorne." She took a moment to take in all the puzzled looks cast in her direction before continuing. "I'm sure that several of them are quite comfortable with Thorne not being in charge anymore. But others no doubt consider my treatment of Thorne as a model of how I would treat them. If I did something drastic to Thorne, they would wonder if they would be next, if I would turn tyrant and banish them too. Their cooperation is contingent on our good will toward Thorne, and Goldenvalley is a better place for it."

"But can't you at least send her away?" Oriana said. "She's dangerous. Why do you keep a dangerous sorcerer around, especially since we apprentices don't have any defenses against her?"

Marlys faced the apprentices, who had sat together in the center of the room. "In the first place, you are less in danger than we sorcerers are. You're the future of Goldenvalley. She knows it. When you were lost in the blizzard, she was angry at us for not keeping better track of you. She feels she can mold you into sorcerers she wants to have around."

Lyra shifted her weight in her chair. "I'm not sure I'd want that."

Marlys smiled. "I don't think that will happen, no. I wanted to explain to you why you apprentices are safer than you might think. Look around at all of us sorcerers. Any one of us would risk life and limb for you. You're protected better than you realize."

The apprentices scanned the room and found the other sorcerers nodding in agreement with Marlys.

"Here's another idea to consider: your future is going out in the world, using your sorcery to help people. Not all citizens you encounter are going to be nice to you. Some are going to be downright mean. You are not authorized to do harm to them, and will be disciplined if you do except under extreme circumstances. Part of your training is to go out with sorcerers to see how they work. You've probably already encountered grouchiness or stubbornness on these assignments. You must learn how to live with disagreeable people, people you don't personally like but have to communicate with, and this is another reason why we have not sent you away while Thorne is here."

"She is very close to crossing the line," Celestine said.

"When she does, we will deal with it," Marlys said. "Another important thing never to forget is that even the nastiest of people have friends, friends who will be angry if you mistreat one of theirs." Marlys inclined her head toward Nessa. "You saw how Nessa reacted when I time-bound Thorne, didn't you? That's just one example."

"An example I now regret," Nessa said glumly.

Marlys nodded to her. "Granted. But you're not the only one. Sorcerer Elspeth has been a great help to us, and, like it or not, she's Thorne's long-time friend. What happens to her loyalty if we mistreat Thorne? What of her other friends among the sorcerers of her own assembly who are elsewhere in Goldenvalley? This is something we need to keep in mind."

"I see your point," Celestine said, "but what do you propose we do if Thorne puts us all in danger? We can't just stand back and watch, and our oath not to harm another sorcerer limits what we do."

Oriana spoke up. "We apprentices aren't pledged." She gestured to Lyra. "Lyra is a good fighter, almost as good as Rochelle."

She was answered with a chorus of loud "nos" from every sorcerer in the room.

"Do not challenge a sorcerer," Marlys said sternly. "Never. We can hurt you and hurt you badly."

"Don't mince words, Marlys." Rochelle leaned toward the group of apprentices. "We can kill you."

"At the very least," Marlys said. "There's the knockout spell. It's in every spell book in every fortress, and it's there for a reason. As I said, citizens can be nasty. In rare cases, someone might come after you with a knife or other weapon. The knockout spell renders them unconscious for a time. They wake up feeling very tired, but no harm is done. Any sorcerer can use that spell on you apprentices…or even other sorcerers."

Oriana turned to Celestine. "You haven't taught us that one yet."

"In due time," Celestine said patiently.

"I only know of three cases in all these centuries when a citizen killed a sorcerer," Serena said. "In all of those cases, the sorcerer was taken by surprise and death was instantaneous: a crossbow bolt through the heart or someone coming from behind and slitting the throat. Injuries can happen, of course, accidental or from deliberate action, but even those are uncommon."

The apprentices' faces showed they had listened attentively.

Celestine faced Marlys. "My question remains: what do we do if Thorne endangers us all?"

Serena took a step forward. "I can stop any sorcerer from performing any spell. Remember when Marlys first released everyone who was time-bound, I suppressed the magic in the room? This is a variation on that spell. It has the added feature of leaving this spell caster fixed in place until released."

Everyone turned to her.

"I'd forgotten," Celestine said. "If it isn't one of those that only a Librarian can do, I'd like to learn it."

"It's one of those spells," Serena said, "difficult to learn, complicated to cast, and not to be used lightly." She turned to Marlys. "I intended to teach it to you, but with everything going on, we haven't had the time."

"I understand." Marlys faced Celestine. "Until then, there's the good old blocking spells we all know. I, and the other Librarians here, can put considerable force behind it."

Tir walked up behind Serena and Marlys and put one hand on each of their shoulders. "Not to mention that while we were at the Library, the Head Librarian said that Marlys and Serena have reached the pinnacle of sorcerous powers."

The faces of those in the room broke out into smiles, followed by extended congratulations.

"Thank you," Marlys said when the chorus faded. "Now, how about supper? I don't know about anyone else, but I'm getting hungry."

Thorne returned to the dining hall in time for supper, seating herself at a table across from the others. Apparently she noticed the surreptitious glances aimed at her: at the end of the meal, she remarked loudly, "What is it? Did I secretly grow another arm?"

Marlys left her chair and sat next to Thorne, facing her. "Remember earlier when you were practicing vortex spells with me and Tir and Serena?"

Thorne lifted her chin. "What of it?"

"That won't be necessary anymore. At the Library of Sorcery, we developed a way to get rid of the ash for good."

Marlys heard exclamations of surprise and delight and realized that she and the other Librarians had not yet told the others of their ash-clearing efforts there.

"Oh?" Thorne sneered. "Another way to bring blizzards upon us?"

Tir turned to her. "No. We used a variation of your vortex spell to collect the ash and force it out into the void. You should be proud."

"Ha!" Thorne said. "I can imagine the calamity. I'll have you know that in your absence, I almost scattered the ash myself. The spell just needs a little more refinement."

"Let us try our way first," Marlys said.

"We need to get this crisis resolved before we all perish," Thorne said. "Someone has to do something, and I have yet to see you do anything productive."

"In that case, you can observe what we do tomorrow." Marlys turned to face the other sorcerers. "Tonight, we'll discuss the plan we have. You can listen if you wish. If it doesn't work, we can talk about next steps."

"Hmph," Thorne said derisively.

"I want to hear about this plan," Celestine called.

Marlys stood. “Good, because all of the sorcerers here will be needed.”

“Not just Librarians?” Astrid said hopefully.

Marlys smiled. “Not just Librarians. Let’s get supper cleaned up and we can settle down to talk.”

When they had gathered again with tea and cakes, Marlys explained the plan.

“The Librarian skywatchers have determined that the best way to clear the ash is to have two main points of action: the Library district in the north, and the mining district in the south. The Librarians will take care of their location. We will send sorcerers to the other: Serena and Tir will take a group of sorcerers from Goldenvalley.”

“Aren’t you going, Marlys?” Lyra asked.

“No,” Marlys said. “Zaria and I will stay here. Tonight, Zaria will send word to the other locations to watch the sky. If the air currents begin to scatter the ash, the sorcerers in the various locations will need to send it over to Serena and Tir.” Marlys carefully did not add that the reason she was to stay at the Goldenvalley fortress was to monitor Thorne.

“We have modified the spells so they are self-sustaining,” Tir said. “So the ash should come to us by itself, but spells don’t always work as planned. That’s the reason we need sorcerers all over the continent to keep an eye on the skies above their locations.”

“In other words, your brilliant plan may fail miserably,” Thorne said sardonically.

Everyone glanced at Thorne before Marlys spoke again.

“Zaria will teach everyone the ash-gathering spell tonight when she relays the plan.”

“Can we watch?” Oriana said.

“I don’t see any reason why we can’t take apprentices with us to the mining area,” Rochelle said.

“I want to stay with Marlys,” Lyra said.

“It’s your choice,” Marlys said. “Each apprentice can decide whether to go or stay.”

“I didn’t mean just that,” Oriana added. “I mean watch Zaria as she gives the instructions to everyone.”

Zaria stood. “Of course. Let’s go to the audience room and I’ll open the sorcerous channels.” She scanned the room. “If the other sorcerers here can join me, we’ll be able to go over the spell ourselves and discuss how we will coordinate our efforts.”

As those in the room pushed back their chairs, Marlys said, “I’ll linger here over tea, if you don’t mind. I know the plan, and I know that all of you can work well without me being there.”

“I’ll stay and finish my tea as well,” Serena said.

Tir rose from his chair. “I’ll help coordinate.” He followed the others out of the room.

When only Thorne, Marlys, and Serena remained, Thorne said, “Not going to monitor your charges?”

“I remind my assembly regularly that they have the power to work independently and don’t need to consult me about every little task,” Marlys said.

“This is not a little task,” Thorne said. “The fate of the world depends on this, as I understand it.”

“Tir, Rochelle, Nessa, and Zaria know everything I do about this exercise,” Marlys said. “There is no risk if I’m not there for the discussions.”

Thorne gave her head a small shake and took another sip of tea. “Incompetent again,” she mumbled under her breath.

Chapter 23

Thorne refilled her teacup from the pot on the table and turned to Serena. "I'm surprised that you haven't assumed a high sorcerership, with all of your powers."

"You never know when it's wise to quit, do you?" Serena said.

"Whatever do you mean?" Thorne asked innocently.

"You know what I mean," Serena said. "Trying to drive a wedge between me and Marlys by attempting to make me feel undervalued and ill-used. It won't work."

Thorne took another sip. "I was merely saying that you, with your celebrated talents, could be a high sorcerer yourself."

Serena faced Thorne squarely. "I did not walk all the way from Majesticacres to become a magistrate. I came here to become a sorcerer."

"I said nothing about being a magistrate," Thorne said.

"A high sorcerer isn't just a sorcerer," Serena said, "as you well know. I've watched Marlys from the time I was an apprentice here. She must act as a magistrate quite often. She must see to the welfare of the entire region. She must assign members of the assembly to various tasks. She must keep records. She is responsible for the education of apprentices. She needs to know who is best to send to the training centers. She must assign those she can trust to carry out the work that she does not have time to do. I would find such tasks mind-numbing. Marlys, who grew up in a magistrate's household, finds these things familiar, she's good at them, and she doesn't mind doing them."

"You could delegate what you don't want to do," Thorne said.

"I repeat: I came here to be a sorcerer, nothing else."

"But you teach spells to others."

Serena nodded. "That I will do. I don't mind teaching individual spells. But educating apprentices requires a singular talent. Celestine, for instance, wanted to be a teacher when she grew up, and also wanted to be a sorcerer. As the primary educator here, she can evaluate an apprentice's strengths and weaknesses, give them the exact instruction they need with those in mind. They all adore her. She, and Marlys, excel at making schedules as to who is responsible for kitchen duty and when, who cleans out the barns and when, and all the other tasks that need to be done in a large household. I have no interest in posting assignments."

"You can delegate those as well," Thorne said.

Serena grasped her cup, walked over to Thorne, and looked her straight in the eye. "Most of all, Marlys possesses the patience to tolerate the stubborn, the obstinate, and the incalcitrant. I do not." After holding Throne's attention for a few moments, she walked away.

Thorne looked down and grasped another cake from the tray on the table.

Marlys followed Serena. When she reached the audience room, she found everyone in a cluster just beyond the door, apparently eavesdropping on the conversation Serena and Thorne just had in the dining hall. Scanning all the faces, she said, "I thought you were going to open the sorcerous channels and spread the word about our plan."

Tir grinned and crossed his arms in front of him. "We will. But we couldn't miss the evening's entertainment!"

Marlys put a hand to her forehead.

Serena laughed out loud.

The next day, after breakfast, everyone left the fortress except Marlys, Zaria, Lyra, and Thorne. With Thorne sipping tea in the dining hall, Marlys, Zaria, and Lyra donned jackets and boots and walked outside. Lyra added thick gloves.

Lyra looked up. "Does it take a sorcerer using a far-seeing spell to notice anything?"

Marlys scanned the skies. "I don't see a change, either."

"They probably haven't started yet," Zaria said.

"It will take a while for the effect to be visible here," Marlys said.

"Can we ask through the sorcerous channels?" Lyra asked.

"We could," Marlys said, "but I don't want to distract them in their work. We'll know soon enough."

To pass the time, they began to walk around the fortress. Facing south, they saw smoke in the distance.

"Is that over at Frosthollow?" Zaria asked.

Marlys cast the far-seeing spell again. "Yes, and there's a fire at a storage building. Someone was probably careless with a lantern again."

Zaria created an end point. "I'll take care of it."

"I'll gather some snow and drop it on the roof," Marlys said. "That should help."

Zaria nodded and stepped through the end point.

Marlys sorcerously gathered a huge amount of snow and pushed it toward the building. When the snow cloud hovered over the roof, she released the spell and dropped the snow.

At the same time, she felt a strong wind at her back. Snow swirled in the air around her.

"Marlys, Thorne created a whirlwind!" Lyra tugged her sleeve and pointed.

Marlys pivoted sharply. The narrow whirlwind did not quite stretch from the ground to the clouds, was not quite a tornado, but still was capable of producing a damaging wind. She cast the appropriate spell to disperse it, and began striding in that direction. When she passed the fortress's western wall, she saw Thorne standing in the clearing there, working to control another vortex, which neared the orchard. Marlys added her strength to quell it, but not before the vortex ripped apart some of the prime fruit trees.

Quickly, Marlys looked around to make sure no other whirlwinds were in sight, then ran to where Throne stood, facing the orchard.

"That was completely irresponsible!" Marlys shouted as she drew even with Thorne.

Thorne turned to her. "It was a mistake, that's all. I tended to it."

Marlys thrust her arm in the direction of the orchard. "What about the trees? You're the one so concerned about food supplies. It will take years for new trees to grow and produce fruit!"

"Most of the trees are still there," Thorne said, "We always gathered more than we needed anyway."

"If the whirlwhind had gone much farther, it could have damaged the fortress or the barns!"

"They're spelled to resist strong winds."

"That doesn't mean they can't be damaged."

"I told you, I stopped it."

"*We* stopped it."

"I could have stopped it without your help. I had everything under control. The orchard was just an accident."

"Oh, I see. When you make an error, it's just a mistake," Marlys said. "But when I make a mistake, I'm incompetent and ought to step aside as High Sorcerer."

"You are not the High Sorcerer here, and never have been," Thorne said.

"I don't care how you regard me," Marlys said. "I'm concerned about what you do. Right now, you're going inside the fortress until the others return."

Thorne threw back her head and laughed before facing Marlys. "Return to what? All they'll do is create a worse blizzard than before. Your only chance is to let me work my spell."

"And create more whirlwinds? No. You're going back to the fortress." Marlys reached out and grabbed Thorne's sleeve.

Thorne wrenched away. "You can't control me. My spell will work this time. I only need to make a slight adjustment now. All you need to do is watch."

Marlys gathered herself to cast a pushing spell. "I've had enough of this."

"So have I." Thorne cast a spell.

Marlys was trapped. She could see everything, hear everything, but when she moved, she met sorcerous restraining walls all around her.

"That should hold you," Thorne said. "I presume you can hear and see me, though I can't see you."

Taking deep breaths to calm herself, a memory came to Marlys's mind. Genevieve had told her about trap spells, which she explained could be discovered by chance when a sorcerer practiced traveling spells. Thorne did not have the strength for a transportation spell, but Serena had said Thorne had been experimenting with the end point spell.

Fortunately, Genevieve had a remedy. Marlys could not see the sorcerous walls restraining her, but Genevieve had said if she used the spell that allowed one to see through thick fog, she could find her way out. Unfortunately, Genevieve never said how long that would take, and Thorne was readying herself to cast another spell. Marlys wondered if she could free herself in time.

From out of nowhere, it seemed, Lyra appeared in Marlys's field of vision, approached Thorne, and punched her in the face. Stunned, Thorne bent over, blood dripping from her nose. Lyra delivered additional punches to anywhere within reach: Thorne's arms, stomach, ribcage.

However, Lyra did not seem to realize that sorcerers could quickly heal themselves. Thorne recovered, pivoted out of range, and sorcerously pushed Lyra to the ground.

"Stay there!" Thorne ordered as she cleaned her face. She turned, looked to the sky, and gathered herself for another spell.

Lyra scrambled to her feet, thrust her arms forward, and used her best household spell to shove Thorne in the back. Thorne rocked forward with the blow and spun around.

"You have no chance against me." Thorne extended her arms and sorcerously pushed back.

Bracing her feet and leaning forward, Lyra said nothing but kept her arms extended, resisting with all her might.

Meanwhile, Marlys, turning her head back and forth between the two combatants and the trap, slowly made progress. She hoped she could get out before Lyra was seriously harmed. Marlys remembered that before becoming a sorcerer, Zaria had gravely injured herself pushing against the barriers at the Mountains of Wrath. Lyra could go into shock from attempting to breach Thorne's sorcerous barriers.

Nonetheless, if Thorne thought defeating Lyra would be easy, she had underestimated Lyra's determination. It was clear to Marlys that Thorne was doing her best not to kill Lyra, but had to use increasing sorcerous force to fend of Lyra's efforts. Lyra stiffened, her face rigid, groaning with the effort. When Thorne lunged forward, Lyra threw her head back while screaming in agony, giving her household spell all the strength she had in her.

Thorne flew backward, landing in the snow facing up.

Lyra lay prone on the ground, whimpering, barely moving. Flexing her fingers, she tried to crawl, but failed to muster the energy.

Thorne struggled to her feet. Marlys noticed that Thorne quickly cast a protective spell around herself. Facing the apprentice, she said, "If you know what's good for you, stay there!"

Lyra turned her head slightly, moaning.

Marlys continued to make progress. Movement within the sorcerous boundaries became increasingly easier. She sensed she might break free at any moment. If only she could get out before Thorne could wreak havoc. Seeing Lyra's struggles only increased her sense of urgency.

As Thorne gathered herself again, Zaria suddenly appeared in front of her.

Zaria smiled. "Making a nuisance of yourself again?"

"Get out of my way!" Thorne growled.

"Here's something you probably didn't know," Zaria said proudly. "Marlys never made me pledge never to harm another sorcerer." She slammed Thorne with a powerful sorcerous force. Thorne flew backward through the air. Snow cushioned her fall. Her protective spell prevented any injury.

Still inside the trap, Marlys's heart sank. Zaria was right. How could she have made an omission like that? But in this case, maybe it was for the better....

Zaria strode toward Thorne, who still lay cradled by the snow.

With Zaria looming over her, Thorne raised an arm and made a quick move. Zaria fell to the ground, eyes closed.

Thorne struggled to her feet. Looking down at the unconscious Zaria, she said, "It seems you may have learned how to cast the knockout spell, but didn't learn how to defend yourself against it."

Marlys shook her head. Zaria, a Librarian, possessed more sorcerous power than Thorne, but Thorne had far greater experience.

Straightening, Thorne inspected the sky.

When Thorne lowered her gaze again, her face registered shock as she found herself toe-to-toe with Marlys.

Marlys had reached the end of her tolerance. Her eyebrow lifted as her voice lowered in a menacing tone. "Now you will have to deal with me."

Chapter 24

Thorne looked at Marlys. "Whatever lighting spell you used to enhance your aura will not help you." She cast the trap spell again.

Marlys blocked it. "The glow you see is a not a spell, but a sign of my sorcerous strength. I defeated your trap spell. You cannot catch me with it unawares again." Meeting Thorne's glare, she added, "I am not going away."

"Neither am I." Thorne gathered herself to cast another spell.

Marlys grabbed Thorne's arm roughly and pulled her forward. "If you're determined to fight, we need to at least distance ourselves. There has been enough damage done here."

Thorne pulled away, but followed Marlys as Marlys slowly backed away toward the snow-cleared path from the fortress to the road. Marlys hated to leave Lyra in such distress. She hoped Zaria would wake up or the others would return from the mining area soon. When Thorne drew even with Marlys, they walked side-by-side.

"At last, you and I settle on who is in charge here," Thorne said as they strode down the hill.

"We don't have to battle over it," Marlys said. "This is your choice, not mine."

Thorne snorted. "As if you ever gave me a choice."

"You have always had a choice," Marlys said. "You have simply refused to take it."

"Your choice was for me to become nothing, a nobody," Thorne said. "That's no choice at all."

"The choice I gave you was to become an equal, a colleague, a valued member of a sorcerous assembly. You chose to accept nothing but a role as autocrat."

"You have not treated me as an equal. You have treated me worse than you treat any other sorcerer at the Goldenvalley fortress."

"I have allowed you to get away with more than any other sorcerer at Goldenvalley, which you would have seen if you had but paid attention."

"Ha!"

They arrived at the intersection of the path and road.

When they turned to face each other, Marlys said, "I don't want to kill you, and I don't want to die myself, but I will do what I need to do to stop you. This is your last chance to relent."

"I'd rather die than suffer another moment under you," Thorne said.

"If you die in killing me, you won't be able to rule over Goldenvalley. I thought that was your goal."

"My goal is the prosperity of Goldenvalley. It will fare better with you gone even if I am gone, too."

"What of Elspeth, Janna, Kelsie, and your other friends? Why not remain for them?"

"With you gone, they will be free to take over."

"I don't think that the future will unfold the way you think it will."

In answer, Thorne cast a push spell. Marlys cast the same spell. When neither moved, she knew each spell had been countered. So, Thorne wanted to live after all, Marlys thought, else she would have cast a fatal spell immediately.

Marlys continued to plunge forward. Slowly, Thorne lost ground, sliding backwards on the road.

Leaving a sorcerous barrier in place, Thorne cast an encasing spell. Marlys cast the strongest protective spell that Genevieve had given her, better than the one she had learned from Elspeth in Goldenvalley. The spell that Thorne had intended to create a block of ice around Marlys to immobilize her, crashed against Marlys's defenses. Ice shards fell to the road.

Thorne dropped her push spell, and Marlys dropped hers. For a moment, Thorne regarded Marlys spitefully.

"Thorne," Marlys said, "let's put an end to this before something we both regret happens. We can talk, come to a mutual agreement."

"I'll never give in to you!" Thorne gathered herself to cast another spell.

Seeing death in Thorne's eyes, Marlys readied herself to meet and reverse a fatal blow. She hoped that the Goldenvalley assembly would forgive her for leaving them all alone. Such a battle would certainly kill them both. At least they would not have Thorne's interference to deal with anymore.

Thorne moved to cast her spell.

Marlys moved to cast a retaliatory spell.

Nothing happened.

Marlys and Thorne stood facing each other in the middle of the road, halted in mid-motion.

"Sorry, Marlys," Serena said. "I had to stop you both at the same time." Serena faced Marlys and cast another spell. "There. You can move again."

Marlys turned toward Thorne, who remained in the roadway, arms slightly raised. She could see Thorne blinking, her eyes moving to watch Marlys and Serena, her chest showing she was breathing, but she did not speak.

Serena, glowing herself, stepped to a point directly in front of Thorne. "It would be wise for you to use this time to reconsider the course of your life from this moment on. No, you are not time-bound, and I will release you presently, instead of in twelve years, not that I'm not tempted to do so. It seems that you failed to remember what I said about my not having patience with the obstinate and stubborn."

When Serena turned to her, Marlys said, "How did you get here on time?"

"Lyra called me through the sorcerous channels and told me to come immediately."

"Lyra...called you...?" Marlys looked up the hill at Lyra's still-writhing form. She thrust an arm out to cast the end point spell, and found that Serena had already done so.

"After you," Serena said.

Marlys rushed through the end point, Serena at her heels. When she emerged at the top, she saw Lyra on her stomach, struggling to get to her feet. Marlys knelt beside Lyra, gently turned her over, and pulled her up so that Lyra was cushioned on her lap.

Lyra looked up at Marlys and smiled. "I'm a sorcerer," she croaked.

Marlys stroked Lyra's head. "You certainly are. And I am so sorry about what you went through to get there."

"It was...worth it." Lyra lightly touched Marlys's sleeve. "You're glowing."

Marlys smiled. "A sign of sorcerous strength."

Lyra smiled back.

Sorcerers and apprentices began to appear around them.

Celestine glanced toward Marlys. "I see you're glowing, too. Serena started glowing after she cast her part of the ash-clearing spell."

Nessa spotted Zaria and rushed to her side.

"Knockout spell," Marlys called to her.

Nessa nodded, put an arm underneath Zaria's shoulders, and lifted.

Zaria's eyes fluttered open. "I feel as if I put in a day's hard labor."

"I'll help you inside," Nessa said. Astrid came to her aid and between them, pulled Zaria to her feet.

Meanwhile, Rochelle had reached Marlys and looked down at Lyra.

"New sorcerer," Marlys explained.

Rochelle grinned. "Congratulations. I bet you feel as if you were trampled by a bull."

"You don't know the half of it," Marlys said.

Rochelle nudged Marlys. "Allow me." She picked up Lyra and carried her back to the fortress.

Marlys stood to see Celestine staring at the road below.

"What's Thorne doing there?" Celestine asked.

"Re-examining her life, if she has any sense," Serena said dryly. "Which she does not." She cast the end point spell.

When Marlys and Serena stood on the road again, Serena walked up to face Thorne.

"Before I release you," Serena said, "you need to know that our combination of spells cleared the ash. Tir remained for a time to watch the results and show the sorcerers there how to close the end point spell once all the ash had passed through. We should be seeing blue sky here before suppertime. Congratulations. We could not have done it if you had not inspired the vortex spell." Serena paused for a moment. Thorne met her gaze, which Marlys hoped showed Thorne was listening. "If you had cooperated with us, instead of insisting that only you had the answer, we'd all be celebrating instead of standing here wondering what we're going to do with you. I suggest that you start working with us instead of against us, because if you get out of line again, Marlys or no, I'll send you through to the island worlds myself. Oh, and I can immobilize you like this anytime I want. I strongly recommend that you never forget that."

Serena cast the releasing spell.

After taking a deep breath, Thorne lowered her arms.

For a few moments, Thorne remained in place, turning from Marlys to Serena, who simply stared back at her.

"Truce?" Marlys ventured.

Throne rubbed her wrists and turned her head. "Seems I have no choice," she said bitterly.

Marlys reached out to Thorne, but Thorne wrenched away. Marlys sighed and inclined her head toward the fortress. "It's almost time for the midday meal. Are you hungry?"

Thorne shook her head.

At that instant, Tir appeared. Smiling, he pointed to the sky. "Any moment now."

They all looked up. The ash thinned, the sky slowly turned blue, and the sun shone brilliantly.

Up near the fortress, the apprentices and sorcerers cheered.

Still grinning, Tir glanced toward Thorne before turning to Marlys and Serena. "Seems as if you've had some excitement here, too. What did I miss?"

While the sorcerers and apprentices returned to the fortress by the side door near the dining hall, Thorne plodded to the front entrance. Marlys walked behind her at a discreet distance, motioning to Serena and Tir not to follow. Marlys saw them turn as she and Thorne walked inside.

Thorne said nothing as she and Marlys proceeded through the hallways and up stairs. When they reached their suite, Thorne stepped inside her bedroom and put a hand on the door.

Marlys blocked her from closing it. "You aren't going to harm yourself?"

Thorne stared at her. "No, I'm not planning to harm myself."

Having used a truth spell, Marlys knew the statement was genuine.

"Can I close the door now?" Thorne asked.

Marlys released it. "Yes, of course. You aren't a prisoner here."

"Am I not?"

Marlys gestured. "You are free to leave anytime you want to. It was my impression you stayed here of your own accord to claim a place here."

"Where would I go? Would any region welcome me? If I left, you would track me, so why not stay here?" When Marlys did not answer right away, she asked again, "Can I close the door now?"

Marlys released it.

Thorne eased the door shut.

After a moment's thought, Marlys hurried back toward the dining hall. As she crossed the audience room, she found herself intercepted by apprentices.

"Marlys! Come quick! You have to help Lyra!"

Marlys charged ahead to the dining hall, where she found Lyra sitting in a lounge chair near one of the tables, a blanket over her lap. The back, seat, and leg rest of the chair had been cushioned with pillows. A cup of tea had been set on the armrest. She looked weak, but not in distress.

"Lyra?" Marlys ventured.

Before Lyra could answer, Oriana spoke up. "Serena told us that Thorne's oath not to harm another sorcerer only applies to sorcerers who are pledged not to harm. You have to give Lyra the oath before Thorne can hurt her again."

Marlys looked around at the company of sorcerers and apprentices in the room. Most surrounded Lyra's chair.

Turning to Lyra, Marlys said, "Any sorcerer can give you the oath, Lyra."

"I wanted you to give it," Lyra said shyly.

Marlys smiled. "I'd be happy to." She grabbed a chair and sat next to Lyra, facing her. Gently, she took Lyra's hand and placed it so that Lyra grasped her forearm. Then she grasped Lyra's forearm. "It's very simple. Just say, 'I swear I will never harm another sorcerer, or my life will be forfeit.'"

Lyra repeated the words.

Marlys cast the spell to reinforce the oath by sorcery.

The apprentices around them breathed loud sighs of relief.

Standing and placing a hand on Lyra's shoulder, Marlys said, "Thank you. You called Serena just in time. That saved me. You did well."

"But I hit Thorne," Lyra said softly. "She'll be angry."

"She isn't now," Marlys said. "I doubt that Thorne will pose any danger to any of us from now on."

"Did you do something to her?" Oriana asked.

"Yes," Tir said. "Zaria told us her part of the story, and Lyra told hers. We haven't heard yours. What *did* you do to Thorne?"

"That needs to wait a bit." Marlys looked over to Zaria, who sat across the table, blanket over her shoulder. Nessa sat next to her. "What about you, Zaria, as long as I'm administering oaths. I seem to have forgotten about yours."

"For which we are grateful," Celestine mumbled.

Zaria lifted her head slightly. "Would it bother you if I didn't take the oath?"

Marlys saw every eye in the room turn toward her. "I suppose that I, too, would feel more comfortable if we had a check against Thorne." She leaned forward toward Zaria. "You'll need more training, though. Rochelle knows many effective offensive and defensive spells."

"I'd be more than happy to teach them!" Rochelle said cheerfully.

"Can't wait!" Zaria said.

"Very well, then." Marlys heard many sighs of relief. She turned to Nessa. "Nessa, I need your help. Will you come to the audience room with me?"

Nessa followed her to the audience room.

Once Marlys confirmed they were not being followed, she said in a low voice, "I'm going to use the sorcerous channels to contact Elspeth. I want you to bring her here, and I want both of you to talk to Thorne."

Nessa shrugged. "I can bring Elspeth here, yes, but I don't think that Aunt Thorne is going to listen to me."

"You don't have to say anything," Marlys said. "I'm sure that you can leave it to Elspeth to do the talking. But I think that your being there, despite your recent history, will help. Who knows? It may occur to you to say something."

"I don't know what I would say."

"The goal is to try to get Thorne to realize that she'd be much better off cooperating with us than opposing us. Elspeth has been nudging her in that direction all along. Thorne may be ready to listen to reason after the events of this morning. Again, all you have to do is be present."

Nessa sighed. "I can do that much, yes."

Marlys smiled and clapped her on the upper arm. "Thank you."

Once Elspeth stepped into the fortress with Nessa, and both had gone to Thorne's room, Marlys returned to the dining hall. This time she did not find eavesdroppers. Instead, she found many sorcerers clustered around Tir and....Durand?

Tir spotted Marlys as she entered and smiled. "I thought I'd bring a guest to our midday meal."

Durand nodded at Marlys. "I understand that you might need a mediator."

Chapter 25

Durand gestured at Marlys and Serena. “Are my eyes deceiving me, or are you two glowing?”

“It means they’re the most powerful sorcerers in the world,” Oriana said gleefully.

“Along with the Library’s Head Librarian, or so they told us at the Library of Sorcery,” Marlys added.

Durand lowered his hand. “In that case, congratulations.”

“Thank you,” Marlys said.

“The glow will fade soon,” Serena said.

Marlys remembered her manners. “Welcome to Goldenvalley, Durand. Our midday meal will be ready soon. Please join us.”

While those on kitchen duty prepared the meal, Tir introduced Durand to everyone. Then everyone wanted to hear Marlys’s account of her encounter with Thorne. Once the food was on the main table, everyone moved to take a seat.

Thorne entered the room, followed by Elspeth and Nessa. All turned in Thorne’s direction as she walked toward the main table. Silence fell as Thorne stopped at a point opposite Lyra. Quickly, Marlys moved to Lyra’s right and placed a hand on Lyra’s shoulder. Serena stood at Lyra’s left and put a hand on Lyra’s left shoulder.

Leaning forward slightly, Thorne said, “Are you feeling a little better, child?”

Lyra kept her eyes on Thorne and nodded.

Thorne straightened. “Good. Sadly, the process of awakening one’s sorcery is always painful.” Thorne met Marlys’s eye. “Marlys will no doubt arrange for a celebration for you once you’ve recovered.”

“Of course,” Marlys said. “All the apprentices and sorcerers in Goldenvalley will be invited. We’ll have a feast.”

Turning to Lyra again, Thorne said, "When I was an apprentice, I punched my sorcerer-trainer. I had a wooden statue of a bear, carved by my grandfather, worn almost smooth by years of loving use. The sorcerer mistook it for kindling one day and threw it into the fire. When I found out and demanded an explanation, she said it was an accident. Later, I snuck up on her and whacked her a good one. I told her that was an accident. She could have banished me. Apprentices should never strike a sorcerer. But, we both pretended it never happened. Nothing was ever said about it again." Thorne lowered herself so that she was at Lyra's eye level. "We can pretend, too, can't we?"

Lyra nodded again.

"Good." Thorne moved to take a seat nearby.

Marlys took the seat opposite Thorne. Serena sat next to Marlys. Elspeth sat at Thorne's left, Nessa at Thorne's right. Durand took the chair next to Nessa. Tir sat on the other side of Durand.

The room began to buzz with the usual mealtime conversation. Marlys heard the clink of utensils against plates. Platters, pitchers, baskets of bread, and tubs of butter and jam were passed.

When everyone had food on their plates, Durand leaned forward a little and faced in Thorne's direction. "I see that we're about the same age. I haven't had the pleasure. I'm Durand. My mother was a sorcerer, too."

The room quieted.

Marlys expected a rebuke or a cutting remark from Thorne, but instead, she answered, "There aren't too many sorcerers our age. Elspeth, of course." Thorne inclined her head briefly in Elspeth's direction. "Some scattered around. But not many actively serving. Elspeth tells me that many of our contemporaries have retired in the past twelve years."

"I'm mostly retired myself," Durand said. "My traveling days now are few. I probably spend as much time healing my own knees and calves as I do for the citizens in my town. And one day, like my mother, there will come a time when not even sorcery will remedy what ails me."

Thorne reached for a bread roll and tore it open. "I have not dealt with anything except minor aches and pains so far, but I've known others not so fortunate."

Marlys noticed that those around her had directed their attention to Durand and Thorne. Everyone else had stopped talking. They motioned for dishes to be passed using gestures.

"I understand that Nessa is your niece," Durand said. "She's a remarkable sorcerer for her age."

Thorne turned toward Nessa with an expression of pride. "Yes, she is. Born to my sister and her husband late in their lives. I enhanced their fertility through sorcery."

"I understand she developed an end point spell on her own." Durand smiled at Nessa before turning back to Thorne.

"Yes." Thorne leaned forward a little, faced Nessa, and nodded. Sitting back, she continued, "Nessa is not only talented in sorcery. She is clever at arranging. Her room was always neat and spotless. She even took her father's ledger, where he kept track of the payments for his carpentry work, and showed him how to better list his income."

"I understand that you became a second mother to Nessa after her mother passed," Durand said.

Thorne bowed her head and sighed. Just as Marlys thought she might leave the remark unanswered, Thorne spoke. "Many times, when a sorcerer is nearby at the time of a death, the family asks us the same questions: Why weren't you here? Couldn't you have prevented this? What good is sorcery if my loved one can be taken from me?"

"I have dealt with those questions as well," Durand said. "Not only that, I asked them of myself when my mother died."

"And I when my sister died," Thorne said. "It was even harder when Nessa asked me those same questions."

"The universe goes on," Durand said, "though it seems at the time that it should stop and go back to the way it was."

"The world can be cruel," Thorne said. "For some things, there is no returning. That is why the Ruler of the Universe and the Bright Beings created sorcery, to make the world a little more bearable."

"I know that Nessa appreciated your presence in her mother's stead," Durand said.

Thorne glanced at Nessa again before answering. "Yes. It was the least I could do. Nessa and her father lived close enough that I could travel there for the evening meal most days. Nessa would proudly show me how she performed household spells and said she would become a sorcerer like me someday."

"And so she is," Durand said. "She made a monumental effort and great sacrifice on your behalf."

Leaning back in her chair, Thorne stretched her arm toward Nessa, who also leaned back and faced her aunt.

"I have been remiss in not expressing appreciation for that," Thorne said.

"Thank you, Aunt," Nessa replied.

Thorne and Nessa returned to focusing on their meals.

When no further words came from either Thorne or Durand, Tir caught Durand's attention by telling him about the Library of Sorcery, especially Blair.

At the meal's end, those on kitchen duty started the cleanup. Most carried their plates and utensils into the kitchen as usual. Astrid took her own and Marlys's plates, then came back to take Durand's. Nessa cleared Thorne's area. Astrid returned from the kitchen with tea and cakes for Marlys, Thorne, and Durand.

Apprentices and sorcerers gleefully assisted Lyra out of the room. Once the cleanup was complete, only Durand, Marlys, Thorne, Elspeth, and Nessa remained. Marlys had already signaled to Serena, Tir, and Rochelle that they need not remain.

Elspeth stood and put a hand on Thorne's shoulder. "I should be getting back. Will you be all right?"

Thorne nodded. "Yes, thank you."

"I'll take you home," Nessa said to Elspeth. They walked out of the dining hall.

For a time, Thorne, Marlys, and Durand sat quietly. Thorne sat with her head bowed, concentrating on her teacup, stirring the tea absently.

Marlys stood and touched Durand's shoulder. "I'm going to check for listeners. I'll be right back." When she found that no one had lingered in the audience room or the kitchen, she resumed her seat opposite Thorne.

Durand moved to sit next to Thorne.

Without looking up, Thorne said, "My guess is that you are wondering what to do with me."

"No," Durand said, "I was wondering what you wanted. What future do you see for yourself?"

Thorne looked up and pointed her spoon at Marlys. "Whatever she wants."

"I have too many responsibilities in my life to manage yours," Marlys said.

Thorne snorted.

Durand inhaled and sat back in his chair. "If you could do anything you wanted, what would you do?"

"I'd be the high sorcerer here," Thorne said in a flat tone.

"And I'd have my mother back," Durand said.

Thorne nodded. "For some things, as we said, there is no returning. This is one of them."

"Then," Durand said, "absent a high sorcership, what would you want to do?"

Thorne glared at Marlys. "I want to be a sorcerer. I want respect. I want to be included in the assembly. Not being watched all the time. Not being lightly dismissed."

Marlys spread her hands. "Easily done."

Thorne drew back her head.

"Cast a truth spell if you don't believe me," Marlys said.

"I did," Thorne said glumly.

Durand turned to Marlys. "What is it that you want?"

"Simply, I want Thorne to recognize me as the High Sorcerer of Goldenvalley and cease her efforts to supplant me."

"Thorne?" Durand said.

"I can no longer resist the universe's will," Thorne said.

Durand slapped the table loudly. "Done!"

"Done?" Marlys and Thorne said at the same time.

Durand turned from Marlys to Thorne. "Done! If you're willing to swear to your declarations, I'll take your oaths."

Marlys turned to Thorne. "We'll have a celebration for Lyra soon. Every sorcerer and apprentice in Goldenvalley will be here. It will be better if we swear publicly, in front of everyone."

"And before then?" Thorne asked.

"In cases such as these," Durand said, "I will take an oath of intent."

"Meaning that we swear that we intend to take the oaths at Lyra's celebration?" Marlys asked.

"Exactly," Durand said.

"I've taken oaths of intent before," Thorne said. "I am agreeable."

"One more thing I thought of," Durand said. "Absent the high sorcerership, how about giving Thorne a title? Such as Grand Sorcerer?

"No," Thorne and Marlys said.

"Elder sorcerer?" Durand proposed.

Thorne shook her head.

"How about Senior Sorcerer?" Marlys said.

Thorne raised her head. Her expression brightened. "I can agree to that."

"So can I," Marlys said.

"Good." Durand had Marlys and Thorne stand facing each other, grasping each other's forearms.

Repeating Durand's words, Thorne said, "I swear that I intend to give an oath that I recognize Marlys as High Sorcerer of Goldenvalley, that I will give her true allegiance as a member of the Goldenvalley assembly, and will retain the title of Senior Sorcerer."

Marlys then repeated Durand's words. "I swear that I intend to give an oath that I recognize Thorne as a member of the Goldenvalley assembly, with all the privileges and responsibilities thereof, and that she shall be given the respect that her experience deserves under the title of Senior Sorcerer."

Durand sealed the oath with sorcery.

When Marlys and Thorne had released each other, Marlys added, "I will have to share this news to the others here, and I will have to do that outside your presence. Is that acceptable to you?"

Thorne snorted. "Of course I recognize that some conversations need to be privately shared among a limited number of participants. I was High Sorcerer here, after all."

Leaving Thorne and Durand to talk, Marlys went in search of the others. She found them in the classroom, planning the celebration for Lyra. They all quieted and turned to Marlys when she stepped inside the room.

"Well?" Tir said after a moment of silence.

Marlys explained the agreement that Durand had mediated.

"Senior Sorcerer?" Rochelle queried.

"I don't care if she calls herself 'Lighting Bolt,'" Tir said, "as long as she recognizes Marlys as high sorcerer and doesn't cause any more trouble."

"Are there any special responsibilities that come with that title?" Celestine asked.

Marlys shook her head. "No. She has the exact same responsibilities as any other sorcerers in the assembly. No more, no less."

Celestine let out a breath. "I can live with that, I suppose."

"Especially since we have Marlys, Serena, and Zaria to rely on if she ever thinks of breaking that oath," Rochelle said.

"This does mean that we stop monitoring her," Marlys said, "that we include her when we confer about regional matters, and that we refrain from mocking her."

Tir dramatically put a hand to his forehead. "It's a sacrifice, but I can make it."

Marlys heard giggles.

"Is this assembly an exception to your rule about including her in assembly discussions?" Serena asked.

"Yes," Marlys said, "and she agreed to it."

"Now that," Serena said, "shows that she can act sensibly after all."

Three days later, all the sorcerers and apprentices in Goldenvalley gathered at the fortress to celebrate Lyra's becoming a sorcerer. The Library had sent Blair as a representative. Tir introduced Blair to Durand and the three shared conversation before the event. Marlys had authorized the release of supplies from the food storage units for a feast. When Thorne asked about this, Marlys explained that she had requested an ample, but not generous, amount.

Word had spread that Thorne would pledge to recognize Marlys as High Sorcerer of Goldenvalley, and that Marlys, in turn, would give Thorne a title of Senior Sorcerer and make her a part of the Goldenvalley assembly. According to Astrid, this agreement had been welcomed not only throughout Goldenvalley, but in the other regions as well.

To further honor Lyra on her special occasion, Marlys and Thorne agreed that Lyra would seal the oath. Durand had coached Lyra in how to use sorcery to accomplish this. So it was Lyra who stood with Thorne and Marlys on the dais in the audience room with Durand standing behind them.

Thorne and Marlys faced each other and grasped each other's forearms.

Thorne spoke first. "I swear that I recognize Marlys as High Sorcerer of Goldenvalley, that I will give her true allegiance as a member of the Goldenvalley assembly, and will retain the title of Senior Sorcerer."

Marlys spoke next. "I hereby recognize Thorne as a member of the Goldenvalley assembly, with all the privileges and responsibilities thereof, and affirm that she shall be given the respect that her experience deserves under the title of Senior Sorcerer."

Lyra sealed the oath.

The assembly applauded and cheered.

Thorne stepped off the dais, finding and embracing Nessa. Nessa held her aunt for some time. Marlys felt happy for Nessa. It appeared that she, at last, felt the return of her aunt's affection.

Durand also stepped away, leaving Marlys and Lyra alone on the dais.

Marlys put a hand on Lyra's shoulder. Both faced the assembly.

"It is my honor to present to you Sorcerer Lyra," Marlys said.

The assembly erupted in cheers. Lights sparkled all around. Snowflakes fell from the ceiling. Marlys stepped back so that Lyra could walk ahead of her to receive congratulations.

Epilogue

After the ash abated and the sun reappeared, spirits rose throughout the continent. The snowfall that winter remained heavier then usual, the temperature colder, but no further catastrophic blizzards occurred.

By spring, food reserves were low but not exhausted. The waycakes had helped. Winter wheat began to grow, and spring was warm. Spring planting proceeded as usual.

News that sorcerers had defeated the ash had spread among the citizenry. In the spring, young people who could use household spells flocked to training centers to ask if they could become sorcerers, too. Four new apprentices had been welcomed at the Goldenvalley fortress.

Within the next two years, the weather settled into its usual pattern. Stores were replenished. Even better, the Goldenvalley assembly became accustomed to having Thorne around, and Thorne, in turn, seemed more moderate in her ways.

One evening, Marlys received a sorcerous communication from Edwina, the High Sorcerer of Briarhill. Southwest of Goldenvalley, Briarhill was Marlys's birthplace.

"We've had alarming events here," Edwina said, "beyond our experience. I need your help."

"Of course." Marlys looked up and saw Thorne standing at the open doorway of her room, attracted by the conversation.

"The town of Riverglen was looted."

"The entire town?" Marlys asked.

"Not every building," Edwina said. "Most of the shops. Smaller ones looted and burned. It was twilight, so most of the shop owners had locked their doors for the night and gone home. Some of those who remained were attacked and injured. One of our apprentices was at a bakery. She had arrived just before they closed for the day. Both she and the baker were attacked. We don't know how long she and the baker were unconscious.

The sorcerers at the training center went looking for her when she did not return at the expected time."

"What did she say?" Marlys asked.

"Just that she saw shadowy figures. Then nothing. Sorcerers put out the fires, assisting townspeople to extinguish the flames. They healed those who where injured. Using lighting spells, they searched the area for the thieves. We had sorcerers out all night. Trackers from the townspeople joined them. Not a sign, not a footprint, not even a trail of stolen goods shed in flight."

"What did the magistrate say?" Marlys asked.

"He and other searchers are still trying to find the thieves. Our sorcerers found and healed others who were injured, but they never saw who hurt them clearly, either." Edwina took a breath. "We are all at a loss here. All sorcerers are accounted for. Those who we know can use household spells don't seem to have the ability to do this. I thought that since you're a Librarian, you may know something."

"I can account for all the sorcerers and apprentices here," Marlys said. "I don't think anyone here has gone there or has any intention to cause this kind of chaos."

"Rogue sorcerers," Thorne said.

Marlys looked over at Thorne again.

Thorne stepped forward. "This is a sign of rogue sorcerers. Outcast or self-taught. The situation will only get worse."

"What do we do?" Edwina asked.

"Call for a sorcerers' council," Thorne looked directly at Marlys. "Now."

To find out what happens next, read Book 3 of The Chronicles of the Library of Sorcery, *Shadows of the Sorcerers*.

www.ingramcontent.com/pod-product-compliance
Lightning Source LLC
LaVergne TN
LVHW010059110826
845155LV00028B/407

* 9 7 8 1 9 3 6 8 8 1 8 0 2 *